All right, *technically she was his daughter...*

But in many countries, he thought, she'd be married right now, having children.

He remembered the previous morning, when he had lifted her up to swing from a tree branch in the park—the innocence of her budding breasts, the suppleness of her waist, her soft, developing fullness.

He remembered the surge of passion that he had felt when he had touched her.

With a tremendous effort, he had suppressed his passion then. He could not deny it again....

THE ADOPTERS
is an original POCKET BOOK edition.

Books by William Hegner

The Adopters
The Drumbeaters
The Host
Three Loose Women

Published by POCKET BOOKS

 *Are there paperbound books you want
            but cannot find in your retail stores?*

You can get any title in print in **POCKET BOOK** editions. Simply send retail price, local sales tax, if any, plus 25¢ to cover mailing and handling costs to:

MAIL SERVICE DEPARTMENT
    POCKET BOOKS • A Division of Simon & Schuster, Inc.
    1 West 39th Street • New York, New York 10018

Please send check or money order. We cannot be responsible for cash.   *Catalogue sent free on request.*

Titles in this series are also available at discounts in quantity lots for industrial or sales-promotional use. For details write our Special Projects Agency: The Benjamin Company, Inc., 485 Madison Avenue, New York, N.Y. 10022.

WILLIAM HEGNER

The Adopters

PUBLISHED BY POCKET BOOKS NEW YORK

THE ADOPTERS

POCKET BOOK edition published January, 1974

This original POCKET BOOK edition is printed from brand-
new plates made from newly set, clear, easy-to-read type.
POCKET BOOK editions are published by POCKET BOOKS,
a division of Simon & Schuster, Inc., 630 Fifth Avenue,
New York, N.Y. 10020. Trademarks registered
in the United States and other countries.

L

for Tony Kastner
& *our Kim Novak Days*

Book One

Chapter One

Winter had flung another massive insult at Manhattan, afflicting it with a recurrence of infantile paralysis. Urban Giles, who thought in terms of diseases, had diagnosed it that way in his first winter in the city eight years before. It was nothing short of infantile the way all traffic and all mass transit became immobilized as though its central nervous system had been ravaged by such ordinary elements as snow and ice and wind.

He had navigated the powdered mirrors of highways and fender-deep spur roads from Rockland County, taking almost two hours on the twenty-minute run to the George Washington Bridge before his studded tires bit into naked concrete. Now he stood at Fifty-seventh Street and Fifth Avenue, in the heart of the metropolis, with no sign of a bus or cab anywhere and the prior knowledge, furnished him by his car radio, that none of the subways were crawling beneath his feet. The ineptitude of all concerned added to his conviction that the big city was run by pikers and inhabited by fools.

A conic swirl of snow-flecked wind rose at his feet and momentarily surrounded him, driving him back into the entrance recess of the building he had just left. It was akin to having escaped the crocodile, only to find himself back in its jaws. He had exited hurriedly, not wanting to exchange weather inanities with any members of the board of directors he had just finished addressing. The storm had fouled all his careful planning, blocking the very votes he needed while failing to discourage the negative members. And, as luck would have it, there had been six present, the required quorum to vote on his proposition. It had gone four–two against him. The likelihood of it ever being considered again was now highly improbable.

Goddamn Emory Seymour, Stewart Sumner and Bob Lynn! Had they been present as promised—and voted as they had promised—Urban Giles Associates would at this moment be out of its financial trauma and on its way to producing another of its lucrative, if cloying, fund-raising telethons.

The cold was as bitter as his mood. He was running out of diseases. He found no humor in that observation either. There simply were not enough good, solid promotable diseases currently incurable to keep his organization going much longer. To add to his distress, the public—the fools who populated this city and now could not even keep it running—had begun to question the sincerity and integrity of his productions. He blamed that on a frustrated Lincoln Steffens named Floyd Jasper. In a series of muckraking articles in the New York *Register,* Jasper had revealed that many of the telethon regulars, major names of stage and screen, were on the payroll of Urban Giles Associates. Their heartrending pitches for donations, which had brought in millions of dollars in a dozen different telethons, were really skillful acting performances. What compounded the felony was the implication that crippled children and adults were exploited to pay the huge administrative and talent expenses of the productions, frequently leaving the victims of the diseases with less than five percent of the pledged totals. It was unpalatable material, disgusting to many, and UGA was rapidly approaching desperation status as a result of the public outcry.

Urban Giles had worked since August on details of this redeeming production, methodically eliminating negatives he encountered, slyly restoring the telethon device to prominence as a fund-raising tool by means of a clever public relations infiltration of the media, devoting long hours to planning an entertainment bonanza that would bury public hostility and overwhelm its apathy by sheer volume of celebrity guests. Additionally, he had gone down the roster of promising diseases one by one, weighing them not for their dramatic potential as much as for the approachability of their governing boards. Hell, he was confident he could dramatize hangnails sufficiently to bring in a million dollars in donations to research a cure. What mattered to Urban Giles was finding a legitimate organization with sufficient board members willing to listen to his kind of reason. And reason to Urb Giles was a slice of the profits. He had found just such a balance within the League for Orthopedic Research. The wooing had taken the entire autumn and most of the remaining budget of UGA. Until this misbegotten morning, it had seemed all set at last. Only God could have stopped him. And, by God, he had. In a strangely paradoxical way, it now reinforced his belief that there was no God—for if there was, how could he have done this to him?

He decided reluctantly the only way to get back to the office was on foot. Muttering, cursing, slipping intermittently, he picked his way along the rutted snow paths of Fifth Avenue, moving in midstreet to avoid the embankments of the sidewalks. There were others bent into the winds, too, faces masked by scarves, their hair matted with ice, but he did not care about any of them, nor did he share their juvenile spirit of adventure and imaginary daring in battling the elements. It was an altogether grim day and he dreaded the prospect of conveying the news he carried to his wife Clarice.

Somewhere in his foraging through the whiteness, soft splashes of neon fell on the snow before him, tempting him into a bar room. Temptation was more than that; it verged on necessity. He stomped his feet, flapped his arms and removed his hat in the foyer before entering the main room. In a matter of moments after that, the warmth of a martini swilled in his stomach. Looking outward now, the day seemed less ugly, even moderately attractive when it was considered objectively, without the meeting. There was a certain temporary protection afforded by its very fury. Pursuers were rendered as impotent by it as the pursued.

He began to laugh softly to himself after the third martini, convinced by now that he would rise like a Phoenix from the white ashes about him. A new plot, a new cast, had already begun taking form in his imagination. He called for another drink to aid the chemistry of creation. There was still the lovely house hidden in the country. More than ever it beckoned enticingly, particularly since it now appeared hopeful, even likely, that he and Clarice would achieve their long-sought goal of adopting two children—a boy for her, a girl for him. He stared into the silver lake of gin, imagining what it would be like to become parents after so long.

The head starter, standing before the bank of elevators, was the only employee on duty in the lobby of his office building. Half-walking, half-falling, Giles inserted himself into the entranceway. Images were unimportant on such a day, hardly noticed.

"You all right, Mr. Giles?" The starter clasped his shoulders as though they were in danger of becoming detached.

"Yeah, yeah. Okay, Freddie. Little too much antifreeze, that's all." He laughed congestedly, his lips loose and wet.

"Good day for it," the starter said. "Can't wait to get off and do a bit of serious sloshin' m'self." His thin laugh was severed by the closing of the elevator doors.

Only two girls were in the office besides Clarice. "Knock off," he told them as he entered. "Get home. No sense working on a day like this."

"Thank you, Mr. Giles," they said in unison. They were gone almost immediately, as though they had anticipated early dismissal. It took some of the joy out of his spontaneous philanthropy.

"How did it go?" Clarice asked apprehensively.

"Zilch," he said, pointing his thumbs to the floor.

"Don't kid me, Urb. I can't take it."

"I'm telling you. Zero. Kaput. No."

"But how? It was all set up."

"The fucking weather. Three of our boys didn't show."

"Oh, God."

He began to weave in a circle, as though his feet were fastened to the floor and his body set into motion. "Come on," he said, "let's go downstairs and get drunk."

She eyed him coldly. "Are you crazy? If the adoption investigators ever see that, we'd be dead there, too."

"Fuck them. Who's gonna be out on a day like this?"

She pulled on her coat slowly, then her boots and a long, knitted cap over her ears. He patted her as he might a pet. "Just one," she said. "I want to hear what happened."

He listened to the rhythm of the bar, the rise and fall of the talk, the bull and the horse of the shit of it flowing freely even on an evening of such climatic aggression. It was amazing how perceptive he was in his sea of alcohol, pooled there in the glacier of the city, ready to freeze over and become paralyzed with the rest of it. His mind functioned vividly, if darkly, swimming like an Arctic jellyfish in the murky chill of it.

"So how come Seymour and Sumner and the other guy didn't show?"

"Clare, I told you already. You don't have to be a genius to figure it out."

"The weather didn't stop the others."

"They live in town."

She shook her head. "I just don't understand," she said.

"Forget it. It's over. Just forget it."

He tuned her out, lowered the volume and tone on

the whine of her, bringing in the conversation around
them to distract himself. It made him feel better, mea-
surably more successful, to listen to the laments and
distresses of those about him. Rarely did he overhear a
bar conversation without emerging with a feeling of
superiority. People led drab, dull lives. His was perhaps mostly precarious, but it was also mostly interesting. And challenging.

"So you shoulda seen me . . . I was *so*
smashed. . . ."

What an achievement! How extraordinary, how individual, how creative, he thought.

"Champagne just creeps up on you," the girl continued with her report. "I must've had gallons and these
people—you should be around people like this, they
were something else—they just cracked up at me. They
thought I was a riot. . . ."

He moistened his lips with the outer shoal of his
martini and probed tentatively for the olive sunk there
by mistake. The bartender—the world, in fact—should
know he took lemon peel, twisted and rubbed against
the rim of his glass.

". . . You've never been as sick as I was. I mean I
was out of it for three days after this party. Nobody
knew I could drink so many Tom Collinses. . . ."

"In the wintertime?"

"What's the difference? It's what I drink all the
time."

He closed the intake vent on his ear and returned to
his wife. She was still not bad to look at, old Clarice,
even when she was angry and worried as she was now.
They had been through many more severe storms together than the one outside. And they certainly had

lived a life together which amounted to more than a running dialogue boasting of states of drunkenness.

"What're you thinking, Clare?"

"About everything."

The alcohol had softened him. "It'll work out," he said. "I've got a few ideas left."

She looked at him vacantly. "I'll drive home," she said.

"I was talking to Elton the other day," he continued without heeding her. "Sounds crazy, but he agrees with me—there aren't any good diseases left."

Elton Richards specialized in forming foundations for the researching and treatment of various diseases, arranging for important backing in names and dollars, then having himself appointed executive director at an impressive salary. He had been one of Urban's prime supporters in the telethon business, involved with him in seven of them. But the muckraking had slashed into his professional sphere as well, subjecting a number of the foundations to budget cutbacks in some cases, to attrition and abolition in others. He was of small consolation to the Giles enterprise these days, fighting as he was for his own survival as head of a minor geriatric research society.

"We should go back to St. Louis," she said.

He scoffed facially and flung his arm outward. "I made a mint in this town," he reminded her.

"No more," she said. "And where is it? It takes a mint to keep anything going here."

"Giles is still a formidable name in New York," he insisted.

The second drink had risen in her and loosened her tongue. "Urban Giles is dead in this town," she said.

He lapsed into silence after that. Later, after a hazardous couple of hours on the highways, they were home in the pre–Revolutionary War farmhouse they had restored with painstaking diligence.

She threw a splash of starter fluid on the logs and then sat back with him to face the licking familiarity of the red, open mouth of the fireplace. "I didn't really mean what I said before," she apologized.

He stared into the tongues of flame and smiled thinly. "Just wait till the kids come," he said. Whatever he meant, she knew she had been forgiven.

Chapter Two

While they waited in the reception area of the agency, behind their facades of potential parent respectability and equanimity, the mind of Urban Giles churned restlessly. Like a computer scanner set free, it roamed the files of his mental laboratory with random selectivity, searching for the combination of circumstances and ingredients which would salvage the operations of Urban Giles Associates.

In his quiet desperation, he had even briefly considered, weighed and then rejected the idea of staging a telethon centering on this immediate personal cause: the adoption of babies. But it was fraught with hazards. And there was the additional danger he and

Clarice would become too emotionally involved. He had a facility for detachment as he was demonstrating to her now. But she was trembling even as she thought of their mission, trying unsuccessfully to hide from him her inability to contain all the mixed emotions of the moment. Still, it mattered little what he thought or observed at this juncture so long as she succeeded in masquerading her true feelings, her real weaknesses, before the screening committee they were about to face. Life seemed in recent months to be all boards and panels and committees for them.

It should have been routine to her by now, as it seemed to be for him. After all, they had endured similar scrutiny from five New York agencies prior to leaping the continent for this interview in Los Angeles. No absolutes had been involved in their delays and rejections in New York, at least not on the surface and not to their knowledge. Yet in three years of relentless investigations and interrogations, they had so far failed to secure even one baby. And they were adamant about wanting two or none. And, as a further delaying stipulation, two of opposite sexes.

An intimate in the foundation business had suggested the California registration. Urban Giles was relatively unknown there. There would likely be less negative publicity surrounding his name there, darkening parental possibilities. All of it had led finally to this midwinter trip—ironically when his fortunes and future had sunk to an eight-year low. But they had followed so many leads and subjected themselves to so many personal peaks and valleys in the struggle for a family they could not abandon the roller coaster now.

Clarice Giles was a small woman with dark opal

eyes and a tendency to add weight when she was frustrated, which was often in recent months. She had been married to Urban Giles for twenty-two years, a childless and essentially loveless marriage dedicated to maintaining Urban Giles Associates, first as a public relations agency, then for most of the past decade as a production firm specializing in charity telethons. It was a slender slice of the entertainment industry upon which to build security. Because of that, there was little real competition—but also little real business. For long stretches of the last eight years, Clarice had been the single contributing being keeping the title of the firm technically plural. Her secretarial abilities, coupled with her acquired know-how in the mysterious telethon trade, had made her indispensable to her husband—professionally speaking.

Urban Giles was a contrast to her. He was what his name implied: urbane, cosmopolitan, clever and inventively persistent. In other words, a city person. He was difficult to be denied when he chose to employ all his weaponry against a recalcitrant opponent or an indecisive potential victim. Tall, courtly when the occasion demanded, but ruthless with equal facility when required, he towered above his wife in both physical stature and ingenuity. She had been his secretary when he was a minor-league advertising executive; he had married her with dual motivation, to gain not only a wife-cook-housekeeper but an unsalaried business aide as well. In every area, except perhaps the sexual, she had satisfied his original projection of her multiple roles. And even there his fantasies had long been contributing to a kind of sustaining operation for both of them. The addition of the children would be certain to revamp and revitalize them as they progressed in this middle stage of their lives.

Every profession has its stereotypes, Urban decided the moment they were ushered in to meet the director of III, the Interdenominational Institute for Infants. She was a brisk, matronly woman of approximately sixty, crisply coiffed and requiring only a nurse's starched white uniform to complete her image of cool efficiency. However, she wore instead a tailored skirt and matching jacket set off by a boldly knotted necktie.

His eyes traveled automatically from first impression to third finger, left hand. To his surprise, it was rung with a delicate gold band.

"Mr. and Mrs. Giles," she greeted them with practiced brightness, "all the way from little old New York just to see us." She held out her hand, fingers downward like the teats of a cow. He milked it perfunctorily and handed it over to Clarice.

"Business is very secondary," he told the director as soon as the preliminaries were over. "The most important thing in life to my wife and me is the prospect of becoming parents of a little boy and girl."

"Mustn't be greedy," she warned with a wave of her index finger. "One is difficult, two is nearing impossibility—and one of each sex is as rare as twins."

Children were the commodity of her profession. He realized that and he had grown accustomed to the impersonalness of agency administrators in discussing their commodity market. But he was disturbed now by a sudden apprehension, his gut chemistry signaling the approach of another dead end, a cross-country wild goose chase seemingly destined to end as had all the

others: empty-handed. He was soured by his own
pessimism even before the long awaited interview had
formally begun.

Fundamentally, they were all the same—the same
cat and mouse intrigues of psychologically oriented
interrogations, little squints and asides, tiny scurries
and pokes, idle prattle strewn with ground glass. He
was annoyed with himself for having been suckered
into a transcontinental washout, no different from those
he and his wife had endured in the East, only more
expensive and time-consuming.

Clarice was reciting the litany of the female aspirant
to adoptive motherhood. Yes, they had consulted medi-
cal experts to determine if there were any physical
hindrances to parenthood. No, there were none apparent. Yes, they were aware of psychological factors and
had subjected themselves to testing, all nonconclusive
and generally affirmative. It was all there, photostated
with the original application. Yes, they had applied
elsewhere before. No, they were not currently on an
active list at any other agency. Yes, they understood
the fee arrangement of the agency and found it accept-
able. No, neither of them was afflicted with any com-
municable diseases, nor had any members of their
families been institutionalized for insanity. Yes, she
believed she would be a good mother. Why?
Well. . . .

Urban Giles shifted in his chair and began a potentially fatal drumming of his fingers on the edge of the
director's desk. He had tested it before and concluded
it was anathema to all people in the adoption business.
Clarice caught it immediately, recognizing it as his
resignation. He had apparently sized up the situation at

III and decided—on the basis of his own computerized projection of results as the networks did for political elections on television—that they were already losers.

He was right. He usually was when it came to evaluating his opposition. However, he erred somewhat in his judgment of her. She proved helpful beyond what any prior agency director had been. At the conclusion of their hour-long examination, she surreptitiously slipped him the business card of a local attorney. "Call him," she said. "He may be able to give you guidance."

Surreptitiousness among people in power appealed to Urban Giles's basic instincts. He called the lawyer, Keith Avery, as soon as they had completed the ritual of adding their names to the general waiting list at III—the "drop-dead list" as Urban called it—and arranged for an appointment the following day.

Avery's offices appealed to him immediately, coating some of his normal skepticism. He was inwardly suspicious of strangers, particularly those illuminated by an aura of success but without tangible verifications. The setup of Keith Avery was decidedly impressive. The offices had more than surface flash; there was an ingrained expensiveness in the furnishings, in the choice of decor, in the turf-deep carpeting, in the choice of wall paintings. All of it was fashionably sparse and elegant in a way he wished for himself.

"A pleasure to meet you, Mr. Giles," he said in a silken voice as they were introduced by his secretary. Urban knew the game. How you played it counted because that was how it was won. Avery struck him as a winner.

"Please call me Urb," he responded.

"Urb? The name here is Keith. Rhymes with teeth," he said, flashing a perfect smile.

A small explosion of static laughter sparked between them, members of the same fraternity sharing a teasing glimpse of themselves upon meeting for the first time. It was a form of verbal striptease familiar to both of them.

"Keith, I've got a problem to present to you. But I don't quite know how or where to begin because I've just met you and I don't know specifically what you do—or what you can do."

The lawyer threw his bronzed face back, a nicely coppered bust of himself, silver colorations in the hair, an even set to the jaw, ready for whatever leading role the studios up La Cienega Boulevard might cast him in. Everyone in Los Angeles with anything going for himself, physically or financially, fantasized movie stardom. Keith Avery was not without his own illusions.

"Would it help you at all, Urb, if I told you I have the III records before me?"

It figured, Giles thought. The woman at the agency was not a traffic cop, directing the flow of her office in beneficial directions, without being a part of the action. She gained another point in his estimation of her, elevating her from an original low to moderately promising high.

"It would help," he replied. "It means you have some idea where I stand, who I am, what I want."

"Precisely," Keith agreed.

He raked back the undulations of his hair, adjusting the even flow of waves as neatly as though a mirror were before him. "Now let's see, Urb," he said. "Our basic problem seems to be divided into several areas."

"The boy-and-girl factor?"

"That's one. But not a major one. If I may be perfectly frank, it's the basic white and basic age desired versus the basic age offered and the availabilities. Or, to simplify that further, the ages of you and your wife in proportion to what you're asking for in terms of children. . . ."

"I follow you, but not entirely. Some of those facts are taken from much earlier applications. There's a great deal more flexibility than's indicated—at least from my point of view."

"If you would settle for a compromise, say, older children, nonwhite, handicapped, along those lines. . . ."

"How old, how unwhite, how handicapped?"

Avery pushed himself back from his desk, pulled up his knees and grew contemplative. "Urb, before we get into all that—before we get professionally pragmatic—I'd have to have your commitment to me as a client. . . ."

"I appreciate that, Keith. I understand it and I respect it. Tell me what it involves, at least minimally."

"You're a pro, Urb. This is always an embarrassment, a little delicate. Especially when you like someone as I do you. . . ."

He was taking the musk of the proposition and converting it into perfume, a process familiar to Urban Giles. He took a deep breath of it, exhaled and proceeded. "How much?"

"A thousand now," Avery said evenly, "the remainder dependent on conditions and delivery."

Urban fished the slender wallet from inside his jacket pocket, extracted a blue check from it and wrote boldly against the dwindling balance in his account, enlisting himself as a client of Keith Avery.

That same afternoon, on the flight back to New York, he persuaded the stewardess to allot him four extra miniatures of extra-dry martinis. The preflight drinks in an airport lounge had combined with the drone of the engines to wipe Clarice out sixty miles west of the Grand Canyon.

A series of quick sidesteps, a flanker move and an end around brought decision to their doorstep faster than they had anticipated.

"What do you say to a boy and a girl, friends but not relatives, both abandoned by their parents? They're currently with distant relatives who don't have the interest or the funds to keep them any longer." He made the proposition over the long distance line as though he were a cattleman, identifying himself after first presenting his stock. "How are you, Urb? This is Keith Avery. I could hardly wait to call you when I heard these kids were available. They're beautiful!"

Clarice got on the extension when she heard Urban return the greeting. Neither of them liked the slaughterhouse aspect of his proposition, but neither of them voiced it. Like most of carnivorous America, they were willing to devour meat but unwilling to face the realities of its acquisition, animal or human.

"Tell us more," Urban said, something wistfully vegetarian about his voice.

"You're on there, aren't you, Clarice? I'm sure you are. Well, here's the story. I think I made it clear to both of you while you were in California that babies are out for you. Too few of them, just a little too old for you as far as the agencies are concerned. Besides, I get the feeling from Urb that he'd really like something a little older, well out of the diaper-and-pablum stage. Right, Urb?"

"How old are they?" Urban responded.

Avery cleared his throat. "She's about thirteen. He's fifteen."

"Wow! Adults."

"Not really, Clare. They're just kids, anxious to be loved."

"They're not in any trouble or anything like that?"

"Absolutely not. Their behavior charts are excellent. I wouldn't recommend them otherwise."

"How long do we have to make up our minds?"

"Not long, Urb. Not with these two. They're really exceptionally attractive kids. They won't last. I already rushed out the full rundown on them to you. With pictures. Airmail special. You should have all the material tomorrow."

"Years waiting and now we have only a day to decide."

"Clare, believe me, there's no decision to be made. I know you're going to fall in love with them the moment you see the photos."

"Anything else we should know before the stuff gets here?"

"That's all, Urb. Just call me tomorrow—the minute you're ready to say yes."

"Thanks, Keith, for the fast work. I wish we'd known about you eight years ago."

"Yes," Clarice agreed.

"I'll be waiting to hear from you."

"I'll call you. One way or the other."

"There's only one way, Urb. Congratulations will be in order tomorrow."

"I hope so. So does Clare. Thanks again."

"Bye."

"Bye."

The information arrived in neatly bound folders, like the prospectuses he had prepared for public relations clients in the past, accompanied by the eight-by-ten glossies which were endemic to the theatrical world. It was all so pat, all so slickly packaged it disturbed Clarice's fragile composure. But she had to agree on Avery's accuracy in describing the children. They were indeed beautiful. They were almost what Urban had envisioned for several years hence. The problem was only whether such advanced children could or would accept the direction and will of foster parents. There was no sense assuming the role without also attaining control.

"You like her," Clarice said.

"Yes," he agreed. "She's exactly what I had in mind."

"He's a handsome boy, too. Almost a man."

They talked about everything all over again and then called Avery. "I told you," he said. "Nobody in his right mind would say no to these kids."

It was difficult for Urban to bring up the matter of finances in respect to them. But it was a deal and it did involve more than the transfer of bodies. "What are the arrangements?" he asked.

"Very reasonable, Urb. Really very equitable. As you can see from the photographs, they're both of Mexican derivation. That does affect the, ah, shall we say charges and expenses involved. In your favor, of course——"

"Straight, Keith. Please."

"Three for him, five for her."

"The total, Keith. All the ciphers."

"Eight thousand."

They sent a check out that night and went to the bank for a loan the following morning. It was all unbelievable and impossible and yet it was. They were achieving what they wanted the way he liked best—under the table, outside the courts, dealer to wheeler, wheeler to dealer. Out of the spin would come a mutual victory: instant parenthood.

Chapter Three

In casting about for a solution to his professional dilemma, Urban Giles asked himself a simple question: What do Broadway producers do with a big hit when it begins failing at the New York box office?

The answer was as simple as the question: They

collect their best New York notices and take the show on the road—to lesser but still large cities, with as much of the original cast and crew as possible. The result: pleasure for the populations of the provinces and a completely fresh, brand new source of revenue and life for the fading hit.

He blamed the distractions of adoption arrangements and the wasted, depressing pursuit of the League for Orthopedic Research contract for not having hit upon this tack sooner. The idea excited him from inception. As he distilled it in his mind, it wound him into a tensed spring, energy escaping from him in streams of words, in restless pacing and hand signals—as though he were fielding ideas striking him from unseen batters on all sides of him; in frenetic telephone dialing, in alternating moods of elation and despair as early obstacles loomed to challenge him.

Circumstances forced the firing of the two remaining girls after the holidays, leaving only Clarice to improvise some semblance of a full production company when Urban was out. It required long hours of application at home, in addition to the office, to maintain the flow of correspondence and propaganda necessary to survival. Necessary, that is, to maintain it in the Urban Giles tradition. He believed in attending to every detail of pursuit and follow-up. Memos and thank-you notes peppered the piles of regular business letters he dictated incessantly from awakening until final capitulation to sleep. It was a high-strung, nervous operation and both of them reflected the strain. The edginess commuted with them to the privacy of their country home, behind the barriers of centuries-old elms and oaks and maples, through the horseshoe hedge rising almost six feet to surround the sides and rear of the house, between the tight-ribbed wooden shutters blinding the first-floor windows. Their life in Elmhill was an odd, incongruous contrast to the sophistication they practiced in Manhattan. "I'd never land an account if they saw the way I hide out here," Urban had said often as they burrowed into the craggy countryside after a day in the city.

Negotiating at least a preliminary holding contract increased in urgency with the imminence of the adoptions. If only he could wangle a letter of intent, with the usual opening retainer of ten thousand dollars, he figured they would be able to manage minimally until June. That would give him five months to either cement the full contract or to move on to new territory. He was ready to move in any direction, wherever events and opportunities dictated.

He had been intermittently studying a huge map of the United States for days when he made an announcement to Clarice. "I'm going to try Toledo. It's in a metropolitan-industrial area, and with Detroit thrown in we could hit a couple million people."

"Yesterday it was Pittsburgh," she said, unimpressed.

He snapped up in irritation, removed his reading glasses, wiped the lenses with a pinch of his shirtsleeve and replaced them emphatically. "I never liked Pittsburgh," he said.

His decision on a target buoyed him instantly. He was never happier than when he was plotting and scheming. With a large map before him, complete with colored pins, rulers and population charts, business was

transformed into sport, a stimulating game of soli-
taire.

She read the elation on his face and moved to join
him, squatting at his side momentarily, finally collapsing her legs in order to sit Indian-style beside his
kneeling figure.

"Toledo's up here," he pointed with enthusiasm.

"I know where Toledo is," she said. "I was trying to
find La Mesa."

"La Mesa?"

"California. That's where the kids are from."

He was annoyed by her indifference to his selection
of a telethon target site. "Forget that now," he said.
"They won't have a home if we don't get this show
going."

She knew by his expectant look what lay immediately ahead of her. He invariably and immediately
followed a project projection with an extemporaneous,
first-draft presentation of his approach to the officials
in charge. As his secretary, he expected her to remember its highlights and show at least a synthetic enthusiasm for its originality.

"Gentlemen," he began on all fours, "as president
and founder of the nation's foremost organization
dealing exclusively in the production of fund-raising
telethons, I congratulate you on having been selected
as the first city in America to be honored with the
opportunity to stage a local telethon rivaling, in fact
duplicating, those my organization has produced so
successfully in New York. It is a tribute to the excel-
lence of your efforts here, in both a cultural and a civic
sense, that Toledo represents the closest approximation

of the nation's largest city among all the metropolises of its general size in the nation. . . ."

His eyes were like those of a raccoon now, dark-ringed and beady, sunken-appearing yet rising within their valleys like small oil strikes in the hills of his face. It was clearly evident that he thrived on the diet of his delivery, even with only a single, jaded listener. "How does that sound?" he asked, taking a poetic pause.

"Do you want me to tell you what comes next?"

He resumed as though her words had disintegrated before reaching him. "I propose to bring a retinue of outstanding Broadway and Hollywood performers—stars, national names, household words—to Toledo to participate in a twenty-four-hour entertainment marathon the likes of which your city has never before seen, alive and in person, and which it may well never see again."

"Urb," she interrupted. "That's mental masturbation. You know we can't deliver a bundle of names to a town like Toledo, for God's sake. We have enough trouble getting them on right here in New York, just a taxi ride away from the studio."

"You have no imagination," he said.

"I leave that to you, dear. What I do have is a little common sense."

"*Common* is the word," he retaliated. He did not like water thrown on newly ignited ideas, particularly by her.

She raised herself slowly, pumping her arms in the air as though they were handles to the jack of her body. When she was balanced, fully on her feet, she left the room, returning a few minutes later with a large martini in a shaker.

"Here," she said. "A little nerve medicine."

He calmed down after that, realization of dependence equalizing momentary resentment. It required effort to subdue the unspoken but recurring belief that he could have done better in his choice of a mate. She, in turn, did not indicate directly her understanding of his vanity. But she did fully recognize it as a necessary force within the ego which drove him. Both of them would collapse if she were to deflate it. And so she permitted it, resisting the temptation to reduce him—to focus his vision more accurately, more realistically, more qualitatively on himself. It was a small sacrifice among many larger ones to indulge his self-image as a latent Lothario, hungered for by untold numbers of women. In a practical sense, it aided enormously in his frequent dealings with female club presidents and foundation board members. What manner of man but a Lothario could stomach the difficult negotiations without the soothing balm of imagining his feminine opponents to be in love with him? Her problem was limiting her own practicality. It interfered with their lovemaking, causing her to question his fantasies with the same tolerance but hardly the same results. They, too, were entwined with his ego, but that did little to relieve the increasing iciness within her.

"Just two weeks," she said as his drink fell to the halfway mark. "Twenty-one years and now just two weeks."

He sloshed the liquid around in the shaker, swirling it upward almost to the rim. And then a hard glint, like sun on cold steel, shone in his eyes. He swallowed the remainder and thrust the tall glass toward her. "One more," he said. "With you."

She hesitated.

"To our family," he added. It had become his newest, most effective way of arousing her. She took the shaker and disappeared into the kitchen.

It did not add up, really, this challenging of one another; the strutting of him, the derogation of her. Yet it succeeded as it always had in setting off a chain reaction. Now there was the additional aspect of the children, progeny without procreation, working upon both of them, leaving them with a need to simulate their roles, repeatedly, seeking to overpower sterility by sheer repetition of the rites of fertility.

He stood naked over the map when she returned, masturbating wildly. "Fuck Toledo!" he shouted. "Fuckitfuckitfuckit!"

The bizarre scene could induce panic in a less seasoned observer than Clarice Giles. But she knew the chemistry of him, the unpredictability of combining elation and depression, gin and vermouth, fantasy and reality in one small unit of time. She placed his drink on an end table, watching as her own frustrations formulated into passion, the virgin and the voyeur renewing an old battle within her.

He was in a crouch now, flailing upward, communicating with an invisible creation of mind and memory. He came abruptly, thick blotches of paste arching before him, splashing onto the map like new lakes imposed upon its cartography. Momentarily exhausted, he fell onto the map, into the reservoirs of his own seas, heaving under the heavy pull of his breath.

She entered the solo now, petting his penis, cupping his testes, slathering saliva over the side of his body, rivering the crack of his buttocks. He had aroused himself, it was true, employing his fantasies to do what she could not for him. But she knew there could be an encore, better than the original, by her own manipulations of his carcass, by sniffing about it vulturishly, threatening to devour it, admitting that appetite and hunger for him were consuming her. It always began as an act, but the role rapidly became the actress and in a matter of moments they were inseparable.

He threw his legs open to accept her, allowing her to mount him, to saddle his crotch, jogging at first, then settling into a steady gallop, her tits pouched over him.

"What do you love?" she demanded.

"Cunt," he said, seeing variations of it in young bodies cavorting before him on the screens of his closed eyelids. The illusion heightened with the release of the word. He swelled within her, the friction increasing for them both.

"Give me a baby," she begged, pumping herself up and down with redoubled effort.

The hot spurts of him sizzled against her interior, bringing a massive climax to the surface of her, traveling like sound waves to the tips of her body, inflating and then puncturing her.

They lay there, washed ashore and abandoned by the tide of their emotions, covering all America by themselves, lumped on a paper map, everywhere and nowhere at once, lost and alone together.

Toledo was not quite the tank town he anticipated. Local administrators, the volunteer fund chairmen in particular, were unexpectedly sharp challengers of his platitudes and generalities. He was careful, of course, not to tread on their civic pride by citing too many New York comparisons. Not unless they favored Toledo. And he remembered to emphasize his own St. Louis roots to lessen his eastern carpetbagger image.

Still, it did not go easily, He was rescued again by his uncanny perception of corruptibility in individuals. One man, a distinguished looking gentleman, caught the interest of Urban Giles from the beginning of his presentation. His opinion seemed to be sought by most of the governing board of the General Aid Fund, which embraced seven charities in the community.

"I think we owe Mr. Giles a fully attentive hearing," he had introduced him, "not just on the basis of his excellent record of achievement in New York, but as a guest in our city. His proposals are before us and they strike me as worthy of our maximum consideration. They suggest a means of sizably bolstering our General Aid Fund in a manner most palatable to the general public, the citizens of Toledo."

It was Gilesian rhetoric and because of it he suspected a Gilesian rapport could exist between them. He sought him out after the meeting, ostensibly to express his gratitude, but more explicitly to learn his name and arrange a private meeting.

"Elliot Ruskin," he returned the greeting. "A pleasure to meet you, Mr. Giles. Your talk was most enlightening."

There was no problem arranging a luncheon get-together for the next day.

By bargaining with the lady in the seat next to him, he managed to get four of the midget martini bottles instead of the usual maximum of two per passenger.

In exchange, he gave her his bags of peanuts, insisting on the barter. The transaction pleased him entirely out of proportion to its significance, perhaps because he was pleased in general with his venture thus far.

Ruskin had been most amenable and encouraging. There was reason to hope something might emerge from the Toledo pitch. However, having been so recently burned in New York by premature assumptions, he deliberately put his thoughts into a holding pattern and concentrated on distracting himself.

His eyes returned to the woman beside him, sliding over her more carefully this time. She was attractive in an orderly sort of way; perhaps more neat and trim than physically good-looking. He guessed her to be about fifty, either in business for herself or an executive with a large firm, perhaps a department store buyer en route to the garment center.

"From Toledo?" he asked with the impersonal familiarity of travelers paired at random.

"Yes," she said. "Native."

He smiled. "Seems like a nice little city."

"Not too little, not too nice. Ever been there before?"

He held up his index finger. "Number one time," he said.

"I'm sure you weren't there on a vacation," she said, lighting her face with a broad smile.

"No," he agreed. "Nice it is, but not one of the world's seven wonders."

Light laughter ricocheted between them. He twisted the cap on the last of his little bottles, pouring the contents over the remainder of the ice cubes, now melted to lozenges. "First visit, last drink," he said in mock distress.

"Those bottles are so cute. It makes it difficult to abstain."

He threw her another slice of smile before dampening his lips with the gin remains. "Ever hear of Elliot Ruskin?" he asked, taking an airborne shot-in-the-dark.

She looked surprised. "Why, yes! What a coincidence!"

"Only name I know in all Toledo."

She turned fully now, taking a much more thorough reading of him than she had earlier. "I'm associated with Elliot in the insurance business," she said. "And real estate."

"Urban Giles," he said, extending his hand without awaiting hers. "I had lunch with Elliot just this afternoon."

"Why, yes, of course. Mr. Giles from New York." She accepted his hand as though it were a gift. "I'm Ruth Fuller," she said.

The subject of Ruskin was brought down from its holding pattern. He was willing, even anxious now, to meet it and hopefully explore it from a new and wholly unexpected perspective.

"What a pleasure," he said. "Please call me Urb. I'm in an informal business. And besides, 'Mister' makes me feel terribly old and solemn."

A Gilesian ploy, he thought, and he watched as she fell for it. "Then I'm Ruth," she said.

"Ruth."

"Urb."

By the time the seatbelt signs flicked on throughout

the plane, indicating their New York approach, Urban Giles had collected enough bits and pieces of the Elliot Ruskin puzzle to assemble a very illuminated sketch, if not a full portrait, of the man. It was difficult for him not to entertain an optimistic appraisal of his Toldeo prospects with the new insight he had gained.

He shared a cab into the city with her, leaving her at the Plaza Hotel with the promise of a dinner meeting later in the week. "You must meet my wife," he insisted. "She'd enjoy you tremendously and I think you will like her, too."

Six days to parenthood and he had all but forgotten.

A sigh escaped soundlessly through his teeth, thin and translucent between the layers of an artificial smile. The business of being charming never got any easier.

"You and Clarice are so much alike," he said. "Talented, independent women like you are the kind men need and want. I'm sure Elliot's as aware of your large contributions to his success as I am of Clare's to mine. . . ."

He was a word polisher, a phrase-honer, adapting his equipment like a tool-and-die maker to fit the problem, to meet the situation. They had knifed and forked their way through the top of the menu, a foreign area to him in recent months, and liberal solutions of gin over vermouth, six-to-one, had sprung the lock on his tongue. Clarice, showing the restraint of experience from a long marriage to a difficult and erratic personality, entered and left the conversation in brief sorties. "Toledo sounds like a nice place," she said innocuously on one occasion. "I've never been there," she said on another. To her credit, she was aware of how inane she sounded.

"You must visit us there," Ruth Fuller said finally, smiling tolerantly. Her airborne abstinence had turned out to be fear-induced and temporary. On the carpeted terrain of Dario's she had already endured three martinis—"Silver bullets," she said in Toledo terminology.

"The more I think about it," Urban said, already wounded by four silver bullets, "the more I think we can exceed ourselves in putting on a spectacular telethon in Toledo."

"You've convinced me, Urb, and I think you've convinced Elliot. I'm sure you can do it. So is Clare, aren't you, dear?"

"The record proves it," she agreed. The room had begun taffying for her, too—rumpling, widening, narrowing, alternately squashed and elongated, clear and blurred, as though she were peering into a funhouse mirror.

"Ready to call it a night?" Urban asked. The act of posing the question indicated his own answer was affirmative.

"Without a doubt," Ruth said.

"I think it's about time," Clarice added to make the vote unanimous.

Outside in the car, Ruth Fuller disintegrated without warning, her body shuddering, her face awash with rivers of mascara and pancake and rouge, a desert suddenly irrigated. It was obvious she had gone beyond her capacity, even exceeded her outer limit.

"What's the matter, Ruth?" Clarice asked tenderly.

"I'm sorry," she blurted. "It's just that I love him."

Urban put together his lines of vision and assembled himself behind the wheel. "Who, Ruth?" he asked to pacify her.

"Elliot," she said.

Chapter Four

The voice came at him in stereo, from all directions at once, surrounding him, intimidating him. Urban Giles lurched from his desk to a window, dragging the coiled telephone wire like entrails behind him. Looking down Broadway, the view was hazed by polluted air, blurred further by the liquid lunch he had consumed to celebrate his recall to Toledo. Elliot Ruskin had convinced his fellow board members a telethon was indeed a tremendous proposition. Would he return, at the Fund's expense, to outline more specific details and sketch out a possible contract? He most certainly would. His mood had been all jubilation that day until the call from Keith Avery.

"I don't understand at all," he mumbled. "The deal was three and five."

"The only way I can explain it, Urb, is that the girl's

relatives had second thoughts about the price. She's a little doll, you know."

"Christ, it's all so slaughterhouse-cold. Aren't they interested even slightly in what's best for the child?"

"They're poor people, Urb. Migrant farm workers mostly. I hate to say this, but they probably figure if they hold on to her a few more years, they can put her into a house in Tijuana and make ten times as much."

"You're making me sick, Keith. It's a good thing Clarice isn't here."

"It's necessary to be pragmatic in this business, Urb. There are plenty of people in this world, too, who are after kids just to have sexual relations with them."

"I've heard enough."

"Sorry. It's just the way it is."

There was a pause in the conversation, orchestrated with a long-distance symphony of electronic buzzes and bleeps, here and there interspersed with faint snatches of remote conversations.

"I'll need at least some sort of tentative commitment from you on this child, Urban. As you can probably guess, there are others interested."

"God dammit. What is this, a slave auction?"

"I'm sure you don't mean that. I understand how difficult it's been for you and Clarice to fulfill your dream of a family. It's not easy for me to report this last-minute change in terms."

Giles tightened the slack within his face and head, trying desperately to scrape the fuzz off the lines so he could gain a clear perspective of what Avery was proposing.

"The boy is definite as things stand. Am I right? Just

the girl is involved? Two thousand more for her you're saying. Right? That makes ten grand in all——"

"It's a small amount really, Urb. Two beautiful children. And you've already given me five."

"Tell you what, Keith Avery. I have a deal to close in Toledo day after tomorrow. I'll get the balance to you then."

"Wonderful, Urb. Congratulations on a very wise decision."

"Thanks."

"I'll have the papers set in about ten days. Can you make it out here then?"

"Have to."

"Good. I'll call or write with the specifics. My best to Clarice."

"Sure. Thanks. If I can just remember to tell her you called."

Avery sent a hollow laugh over the three thousand miles. It emerged even emptier in the ear of Urban Giles. The attorney had managed to eviscerate the joy from the Toledo prospect. Even it now seemed vacant —and far less certain than it had only hours before.

Ruskin was at the airport to meet him this time, very cordial and helpful. He moved him along the corridor after they had claimed Urban's luggage, steering him into one of the bare, overly lit rooms which pass for cocktail lounges in most airports.

"Surprise," he said pleasantly as they came upon Ruth Fuller seated at one of the tables.

"Ruth, how nice to see you," Urban said genuinely. He pointed at her the way people do when suddenly and unexpectedly confronted by a celebrity whom they know only by face.

"Urban! Elliot's really surprised me this time. I thought we were meeting an insurance rep from Hartford." The imprint of surprise on her face verified her words.

Ruskin was pleased by the success of his caper. "I thought you two old friends would enjoy a little reunion party," he said.

They had a single round of drinks in the cafeteria setting of the airport bar. Ruskin had arranged for dinner at his country club some seven miles beyond the field. He was anxious to impress his out-of-town guest with the food and service there. And, of course, his stature as a member.

It was "Yes, Mr. Ruskin," "No, Mr. Ruskin," "Certainly, Mr. Ruskin," from the moment the parking lot attendant placed his glove on the door handle of the car. Urban liked all of it. Prestige. Respect. He gave good marks to people on just such details.

The club itself was a white baguette in a sea of rolling green. Its siding and emerald shutters were as neatly maintained as the golfing greens and fairways. The overall effect was that of a lavish estate, perhaps the home of a multimillionaire with a passion for order amidst elegance. Their table overlooked the approach to the eighteenth hole. Fresh roses crowned the table, rising from regal linen and surrounded by heavy sterling settings.

"Lovely, Elliot," Urban said before the first cocktail had been served.

"Thank you. It does beat McDonald's, doesn't it?"

Ruth laughed appreciatively. "Elliot knows my secret passion for cheap hamburgers," she confessed.

Drinks arrived during the idle bantering, glasses frosted with the silver residue of careful chilling. Urban let himself go, relaxing the tight hold he usually kept on himself during business meetings, whatever their guise. He wanted to forget the hysterical, near-breakdown of Clarice over the news from Avery. "They're not going to let us have them," she had repeated over and over despite his reassurances.

Ruth watched him as he unwound, intently but not obviously. He had not yet earned full clearance from her and her feminine intuition demanded to know why.

"I'm sure we can put on one helluva show in Toledo," he was saying as she surveyed him in the pale light. His face had been pulled back by too many sudden shocks, too many unexpected confrontations and disappointments, until it had become taut and wrinkled at the uneven places—around his eyes, his mouth and below the dip of his chin. He retained a kind of dissolute handsomeness in spite of it all, the overhanging roof of hair resembling city-sooted snow, grayish more than white, a shade approaching raw iron ore.

By the time dinner arrived—a mammoth Chateaubriand—all three of them bore the early traces of excess, lips overly moist, a flush to their cheeks, eyes seemingly drowning in pools of water surrounding them.

"So how can we work out this whole proposition?" Elliot asked, bobbing in and out of the captain's serving choreography. "I mean, of course, in a way that will benefit everyone concerned."

Urban liked that kind of talk. He had overcome the martini paranoia afflicting him on the plane and was back in loose control of himself. "The way I see it, Elliot," he said, "and Ruth here, naturally I mean you, too . . . I'll submit a list of major names, and I mean top stars, not ingenues and featured players, who'll form the nucleus around which we'll build a twenty-four-hour entertainment marathon. You and the board can pick from that list—say a dozen names—and then we'll flood the media in this area, Detroit included, for weeks beforehand. The idea is to make our telethon *must* viewing for everybody in this Ohio-Michigan area——"

"Only a dozen stars? That's two hours apiece on camera."

Urban smiled tolerantly. "You must have an army of local talent who'd give their eye teeth to be part of the show. They'll do a lot of the ballyhoo, too, on their own programs . . . and we'll get the mayor and the high school bands and the beauty contest winners and the washed-up athletes and . . . just leave that up to me, Elliot. That's my business. Believe me, I do know what I'm doing."

"Sounds terrific," Ruth said as she bowed into a slice of pink steak impaled on her fork.

"The stars will be used like prods when the donations get slow," Urban continued. "We'll keep a couple of the big ones in reserve all night to force people to stick with the show. The others will come in and out, making their sympathy pitches, answering phones, hustling the big contributions. . . ."

Ruskin smiled as he blotted his lips with a full fold of napkin. "I like the sound of it, Urban. I know it's impossible to be specific, but just in a very general kind of way, how much do you think we could take in if we went ahead with it?"

Urban leaned back in his chair, rumpled his napkin and placed it slowly, dramatically on the table next to his plate, as though he were a judge with a gavel about to render a profound verdict. "How does a million and a half dollars sound?" he said softly, letting the words make their own noise.

Ruskin touched the table as if to balance himself. "I'm assuming you're serious, Urb. That is a tremendous amount of money to collect in just one day's broadcasting. It's more than the Fund has totaled at any one time in its history."

Ruth Fuller sat immobilized, food still waiting in her mouth.

"I didn't arrive at that sum on the spur of the moment, Elliot. I'm sure you understand I'm a professional in my field and I don't toss out seven figures recklessly without understanding their significance."

"I'm sure of that, Urb. That goes without saying. But aren't you possibly confusing Toledo with New York, or at least with a much larger city than it is?"

"You have a metropolitan broadcast range encompassing a very large urban area. Many of the Detroit companies, the big automobile manufacturers in particular, have employees and suppliers from this town. Even plants here. It's good public relations, good business, to kick into such a highly publicized charity drive as the one I propose to stage for you. They can pull six figures out of their advertising budgets and never feel it."

Conversation was exchanged like chips in a poker game throughout the rest of the dinner. They retired to the cushioned comfort of a patio lounge for after-dinner drinks. It was there, with one appetite satisfied and another whetted, that Urban Giles made his move.

"Elliot," he said intently, "I would go into this only if I knew I could count on your full support and assistance. I'm a stranger here, but in the short time we've known each other, I feel that I've made a good and lifelong friend. . . ." He turned to see if Ruth had emerged from the ladies' room and was relieved to see she had not.

"Thank you, Urb. I'm flattered by what you've just said, particularly because I feel the same way about you. I don't just like *what* you say either, I like the *way* you say it."

Urban flashed a smile, hesitating just long enough to convey his acceptance of a mutual admiration bond between them. "The only problem, as I see it, is whether a majority of the board——"

"No problem," Ruskin interrupted him. "I can deliver the votes."

Urban went for the lock. "This will take a lot of your valuable time and effort, to say nothing of your contacts in the city, Elliot. It's only fair that you receive a percentage of the gross, as is customary in such situations, as a small recompense——"

Ruskin smiled thinly. Question marks formed at the corners of his mouth. "I couldn't do that, Urban."

"You most certainly can. In fact, I won't have it any other way. That's how I do business."

Ruth returned, bisecting their small circle. Her reentry did not disturb Urban now. All the points had been scored. "You boys look like you've been plotting the overthrow of the government," she said lightly.

They smiled in unison, eyes meeting on the same wave length.

"At least," Urban said.

Chapter Five

Thank God for credit cards, he thought. The trip to Toledo would have been impossible without one. Expenses paid always meant *after,* not before. Now he was en route to Los Angeles with Clarice, also on the golden arm of his air travel card.

Ruskin, bless him, had come through with the promised affirmative vote. Even more importantly, he had engineered a ten-thousand-dollar advance on the contract. Little did he realize he had bought a girl with half of it.

Avery, damn him, had been reluctant and bitchy about waiting until the last moment to receive the balance of his money. Urban had employed all of his persuasive powers, exploited the rattled nervous condi-

tion of Clarice, and delivered a photostated copy of his
Toledo pact to convince the attorney of his sincerity,
his resolve, and most importantly, his solvency. Somehow it had worked. And now, at long last, though still
scaling another mountain, they were finally to realize
the summit of one that had defied them for years.

"Got to have one, Clare," he insisted in midflight as
the stewardess stood over them, awaiting their cocktail
order. "After all, this is a very special, extraordinary
occasion."

"All right," she said without enthusiasm.

They were flying coach, which meant he had to
mark their preference cards and pay a dollar apiece for
the drinks. He checked the tiny box next to "Extra-Dry
Gin Martini" twice on each card.

She returned to life with the first drink, a dried
sponge fingered by shoots of liquid. The hardness left,
too, and she felt softer toward him and the tense life he
had led her into. "I hope they're good kids, that's all,"
she said for no particular reason beyond reestablishing
contact with him.

"At those prices, they better be."

"Promise me something, Urb," she said with sudden
intensity. "Promise me you'll be gentle with her."

His eyes emptied. He stared at her vacantly. "What
is that supposed to mean? What do you think I am,
anyhow?"

"I'm sorry," she said.

"I'll be goddammed," he said.

She turned and peered out of the window, not wanting to talk anymore. The clouds about the plane were
like huge drifts of goosedown and she wished silently
she could fall among them and sleep a long time, until

it was all over between them and the lawyer and the children.

Avery sent a station wagon to the airport for them. The driver was a friendly young man, obviously not a professional chauffeur in either dress or manner. "I'm in my last year of law school at UCLA," he explained. "I'm working for Mr. Avery as a legal assistant."

They went directly to Avery's office and were ushered in without preliminary formalities. As a man accustomed to sweating out client fees, Urban understood the urgencies.

"Clarice and Urban," Avery greeted them. "How nice to see you both again."

Urban dug immediately into an inner jacket pocket and produced an envelope. "Hello, Keith, and here you are, Keith," he said with forced flippancy.

"Hello, Mr. Avery," Clarice said.

He took the envelope and placed it on his desk without opening it. "Thank you both. It could have waited." There was still a night to go through before the actual delivery of the children—plenty of time to check its contents.

"How about a little champagne for the new parents?" Keith suggested.

"Tomorrow," Urban said. "Tomorrow's the day for celebrating."

The lawyer lifted his finger in mock protest, wagging it negatively. "Uh-uh. Tomorrow you have responsibilities. I expect you both to be on your best behavior then." He winked to insure he was not being taken seriously. "How about a little of this?" he asked, hold-

ing aloft a dusty bottle from the cabinet near his
desk.

They agreed, with some reluctance on Clarice's part.
Avery gave a small historical dissertation on the cognac
he was serving before segueing into details of the day
ahead. "Maria and Ramon will meet us at Disneyland," he said. "I use it often because it's a pleasant
environment for the transfer of authority with children.
They'll be left with one of my assistants and I'll disappear with her after we've introduced you to them.
They're looking forward to a day at the park and I
think it'll provide both of you with as nearly perfect a
setting as is possible under the circumstances."

The slight hostility they had felt toward him dis-
solved with his description of details. He sounded for
the first time as though he had some compassion for the
human commodities of his profession. And both of
them liked the amusement park arrangements.

"I've taken the liberty of registering you at the Century Plaza. I'm sure you'll find it satisfactory. Unless
you have an objection, I'll come by to pick you up at
eleven A.M. We'll have a bit of lunch at the hotel and
then drive out to the park. How does that sound?"

"I like it," Urban said.

"Clarice?"

"It sounds fine to me. I don't really know what I'm
thinking these days."

Avery smiled indulgently. "Tomorrow night you'll be
moved to a suite so there'll be sufficient beds for the
whole Giles family. I'm assuming you still plan to leave
for New York the following day?"

"Right," Urban said. He had begun to betray some
small signs of the same nervousness afflicting Clarice

now that only one more turn of the clock stood between them and the children.

"I hope you'll excuse me if I leave you now," Avery
said, his voice shifting into higher gear. "I have a client
waiting in the outer office. Take your time, have another drink, and I'll see you early tomorrow."

He was halfway through the door when he turned
suddenly. "I almost forgot," he said. "Good luck and
good health to both of you—to all of you. And much
happiness."

Their tops whirling, the haze of motion drawing
halos about them, everything spun, nothing tangible
outside their own bodies, they flywheeled and pirou-
etted, skated and waltzed into the never-never land of
their fantasies.

Avery was a pro. Because of that, Urban Giles
accepted the drugging martinis at lunch, forcing them
upon his wife as well. They were sedatives, the attorney said, necessary to conquer the ordeal ahead. Clarice was as uptight as he, and vice versa. For two
alleged sophisticates, two life gamblers, the moment of
truth was unexpectedly intense.

"Linda will introduce you," Avery said, waving
passes at uniformed robots, angling into an exclusive
interior parking area. He had obviously been through
it all before.

"Who is Linda?" Urban asked.

"Linda Saxon. She's my assistant and a sweetheart.
You'll love her."

He abandoned them at the lot, a calculated move he
had not informed them of in advance. They accepted it
as the maneuver of a professional. Now wholly within

a gingerbread world, every miniature of childhood distended beyond life-size, all contact with reality slipped like blood from the cuts of a papier-maché sword. It was difficult to translate worry and apprehension into meaningful terms in the bright and carefree kingdom of childhood.

Linda seemed conjured, appearing out of nowhere before them, elfin in a soft suede suit. "Mr. and Mrs. Giles," she said sweetly, "I'm Linda."

They were like figures marching out of a cuckoo clock by now, extending arms, bowing, smiling, and nodding as though their hour had come. "Yes, Linda," he said automatically. "It's nice to meet you."

"Your children are waiting for you." An incandescent smile lit her face without flickering. Part of the treatment, Urban thought remotely, but it was not a time for cynicism and he discouraged his own thought.

Maria and Ramon shared the same sidewalk bench. They were larger, even from a distance, than either Urban or Clarice had imagined. Somehow the word *children* implied miniature. They were both simultaneously taken aback by the degree of their development. The photographs had simply not conveyed it.

The moment was one of extreme delicacy for all concerned. Urban had only to reflect on his own troubled childhood—the aloofness of his father and the alcoholism of his mother—to gain empathy with both of them. And Clarice, failed aspirant to motherhood, middling wife, was flooded with a complex of emotions.

Linda utilized the short walk to the bench to inform them that they would be introduced as Mr. and Mrs. Giles. It would be up to them to establish any future identification as Mom and Dad or Clarice and Urban or whatever.

Then they were before them, their love purchases, tangible at last, tactile, soft, elastic, pliable and possessable. Clarice was reduced to tears immediately. She fell lightly upon the girl, sinking her fingers into her hair, pulling her face to her bosom, whispering, "Little Maria, we love you."

Ramon had already learned the basics of manhood. He stood up, shoulders back, suppressing his emotions, reciting the brief, rehearsed speech someone had taught him somewhere during the hours preceding this moment. "Mother and Father Giles," he said, "I am happy to know you and I thank you for taking me as your son and Maria as my sister."

Many minutes passed before any of them realized Linda had gone. All at once, in the synthetic environs of a commercial fairyland, they had become a very real family.

They were forced to concede Avery had managed the transference of authority in a most gentle and humane way, considering the crassness of his demand for additional money. The beef-on-the-hoof attitude was missing. There was none of the cold quality of post-auction delivery of cattle he had feared. Linda Saxon had been pleasant and discreet. She had taken professional care not to ingratiate herself so thoroughly with the children that they would experience a further sense of loss in her departure.

Clarice assumed the role of motherhood as he anticipated, as though she had rehearsed it a lifetime. There were no surprises there. But the girl was more than he

had allowed himself to expect. Her eyes were dark
olive, her black hair parted in the middle, falling to
each side evenly, like pages of an open book. Her
smile, flashed against a light cocoa face, was almost
blinding in its brilliance. She was shy and hesitant, but
one could not look at her without sensing friendliness
just below the self-protective surface.

Ramon was ever so slightly darker than Maria, his
hair also jet black and gleaming in the afternoon sun.
Through his sport shirt, open-necked, the outlines of a
sleek, well-molded torso suggested a lithe figure already
adjusted to puberty. A contained vitality brimmed
about him, set at any moment to jump or run or climb.
He drew back, in a typically boyish reaction, from
Clarice's effort to kiss him, accepting her hug instead as
an opening act of affection. Urban made it easy on
him, extending his arm for a man-to-man handshake.
"Put it there, Ray," he said. "I'm proud to be your
dad."

An orgy of sodas and frozen custards and jelly apples and cotton candy followed the brief introductory
ceremonies. No one was truly comfortable, no one
sought to prolong the ordeal. All four of them welcomed the distractions of Disneyland as a gradual
means of becoming acclimated to one another.

The sun had begun to slip beyond the rim of the
horizon when they finally admitted they had seen
enough, done enough, eaten enough. An adventure lay
before them, but also an inevitability. Now it would
have to be faced the way it was, without the pleasant
past and the faraway future projected by an amusement park. From here on there was only the present,
stark and real.

They picked their way in the rental car, from parking lot to freeway, feeding intravenously like a corpuscle into the stream of cars heading for Los Angeles proper.

"So, what's the name of my new little girl?" Urban asked as they rode.

"Maria Giles," she said, sweetly and clearly.

"And the big fellow next to you—what's your name, pal?"

"Ramon," he said. "Ramon Giles."

At the sound of the declarations, Clarice's eyes brimmed again. For the first time in all the months of anguish, she knew they had gotten a bargain.

Winter still reigned over Elmhill and the rest of New York State when they returned. The children were enchanted by the snow surrounding the house, the first they had ever seen, but the chill climate was another matter. They shivered constantly despite the furry warmth of their outer garments.

In spite of the temperature, they adjusted rapidly to other factors. School in particular. Despite the provincialism of the town, compounded by their undeniable traces of Spanish ancestry, they were accepted readily by most of the other children. They were both attractive, after all, modest and cooperative in their shy ways. And they had come from the magic land of California, which most of the others had only heard of and never visited.

School enrollment forced the Giles' to assume a more obvious role in the community. It was the single most disturbing element of their new parentage. Their home had been chosen carefully for its seclusion, for its relative isolation close to the city. Urban Giles Associates, as an enterprise, forced the practice of charm and conviviality as a business component. Neither Urban nor Clarice cared to translate it to their home life. Now they had school bus drivers and teachers and parents' meetings and classmates of their children with whom to contend.

Urban was fortunate in that his expanding Toledo involvement began to occupy him more and more. It left the period of adjustment mostly to Clarice. He replaced her temporarily in the office with the same two women he had laid off earlier in the year. They were working as office temporaries when he summoned them, spoiled forever for ordinary employment by the show-business angles learned at U.G.A. It took only two phone calls and a raise of ten dollars per week over their former salaries to lure them back.

There was a dangerous smoothness to his life for the time being and its serenity troubled him. That state had always been ominous in the past and had made him wary. Fate was a sensuous temptress, difficult to escape and impossible to deny. He forgot the pledge he had made to her—to limit his drinking in front of the children. The night of their great confrontation he had careened up the long drive, shearing off a large section of carefully nurtured hedge cover. He sat for a while in the darkened car, collecting himself, drawing on reserves of strength and balance to extricate himself from the forest of brush pressing against its sides. Finally, unable to devise an alternative, he pushed open the door, never thinking to go forward or reverse, simply accepting the car's crowded resting place as final for the night.

The branches made firm contact with him as he emerged, brushing the surface of his skin, indicating a willingness to cut more deeply if he insisted on resisting. When he had the tangle solved, proved by his ability to move his arms freely, he marched up the rolling gravel of the drive toward the lighted house.

She was on the porch, her face curdled in the shallow light. It was difficult for her to be violent, particularly with him. She had always rather mothered and protected him. But now she *was* a mother and the responsibility of the assignment supplanted whatever fantasy role she had played in the past. All the emotions which had been swimming within her seemed to have washed ashore at once on the beach of her face.

His eyes settled upon her like headlights climbing over a hill, ranging upward at first, then falling swiftly, if unevenly, on the obstacle before them.

"Get the hell away from here," she said, her voice low and menacing. His march continued, undulating but undaunted.

"I'll call the police," she warned.

He stopped now. The upswept eyes traced the outline of the house, noting the slice of shade peeled back in the second-floor room assigned to Maria.

"I mean it, Urb. Go away until you're sober. Go back to New York. Go anywhere. But don't come a step further. . . ."

Scrabble was the game his head was playing. He knew the right words to fire back. But where were they? He shook his head, tilting the mechanism, scrambling the letters once more. "I'll take the kids, god dammit," he shouted. A cheap shot, he thought to himself in spite of his anger and confusion. Unwarranted and beneath his intelligence.

She fled at the suggestion. The clear snap of the main door's lock-bolt echoed in the night stillness. A moment later all the lights were extinguished. Standing there alone, moving centrifugally from the base of his feet, snorting the crisp black air, he fought for some deeper comprehension of what was befalling him. What have I done? I break my balls for this bunch and they lock me out. He started forward again, continuing until the memory of the word "police" moved into recollection like a link in a chain. He stopped and reversed direction.

Gunning back and forth, he finally got the car out, shredding several feet of bush. He nosed it out onto the road feeding into the main highway. The car clock registered ten-fourteen. It was as reliable as a sundial on an overcast day. Still, it seemed likely it was before midnight.

At the Holiday Inn several miles southeast, he entered credit-card heaven once more, accepting a maximum-rate room before adjourning to the bar. There, his largesse bought him the sympathy and respect he was seeking. He slept fitfully later, but was undisturbed by the strange environment. After all, he had spent a good portion of his life bedded down in unfamiliar places, sleeping off the remains of still another lost night.

Chapter Six

"I've got to fuck her," he decided aloud and alone. It was a decision based upon necessity. "I have to go to bed with her, god dammit," he rephrased himself.

It would have to be done on his next visit to Toledo. This was a practical matter, devoid of romance or even minimal sexuality. Elliot Ruskin simply was not taking care of his extracurricular duties with Ruth Fuller. He deduced its cause as a demanding upturn in homework. With a wife of only thirty-seven, three children by this second marriage and two from his first, he was undoubtedly being called upon constantly, with depleting demands on his physical resources. Urban understood it even though he did not appreciate the subtle responsibility it was imposing upon him.

Based on his own home situation, he should have a potential backlog of firepower at his command. But he knew such potential was only that; it could not be stockpiled. Otherwise, he reasoned in jest, religious celibates and other abstainers might eventually propel themselves into orbit on the strength of a single, massive ejaculation. The humor of it was short-lived. There was no joking away the increasing pressure Ruth was subjecting him to with each successive visit to her city.

Clarice had all but hidden the children from him since his bushwhacking exhibition. They were kept busy outside the house whenever his schedule permitted prolonged stays at home. She spent her own nights sleeping in the small guest room when he was present, even changing the sheets on the bed they had once shared for each of his stays. He had been through it all before with her, but never with children involved. It embittered him after the difficult transaction to obtain the children and he retaliated by drinking more frequently and fully than ever.

As expected, almost dreaded, Ruth picked him up at the airport, apologizing for Elliot's inability to meet his plane. The two of them had become his liaisons with the telethon base, making escape from her not only impractical but impossible. He would have to escort her to dinner, as usual, but without the saving presence of Elliot. It had happened that way three times in a row now.

"Would you care to go to dinner?" he asked, because there was no alternative. In fairness to her, he admitted she was a charming and interesting companion. It was really only the matter of physical involvement which had begun to pall their meetings.

"I not only care, I insist." She laughed gaily at her own response.

He forced a smile. "I'd hoped you'd say that," he lied. In the back of his mind was the remembrance of a recent night together when she confessed the whole background of her relationship with Elliot Ruskin. He wished somehow he had never learned it. "We started

out as boss and secretary," she said then, the ring of it
familiar to him. "He was married to his first wife . . .
promised to divorce her and marry me . . . then, after
ten years of stringing me, he married this other girl."

She had become too involved by then, she explained, both in business and personal affairs simply to
indulge her self-pity or seek a new life of her own. It
had been touch-and-go ever since, sometimes warm
and tender, more often just business interspersed with
companionship and flecks of nostalgia. He had urged
her to find someone; she had tried but found all of
them wanting in comparison to Elliot. So there it was.
Take it or leave it. The problem was she had lately
found some bases for comparison in Urban Giles.

As if telepathy had reported his decision, her image
changed for this encounter. Instead of her usual busi-
ness-oriented wardrobe, she met him dressed the way a
matron on the make likely would be dressed: deep
décolletage to emphasize the ripeness of her bosom, the
vintage quality of its components. Her hair was coiffed
with a soft serenity about it, a quality few younger
women could achieve because of the contrasting narcis-
sism and impertinence of their faces. She was a handsome woman, not a pretty or beautiful one, with a gift
for accentuating her best features.

He wished vaguely somehow as they met that he was
the kind of man who was attracted to this very special
kind of woman. Her nicety deserved a better reward
than what he planned to offer her. Although he was a
gifted actor in his own field, even capable of faking it
reasonably in others, there was one area of male en-
deavor in which no man could simulate real interest.

Because of what she was, he hoped for a miracle while anticipating far less.

"You look lovely tonight," he heard himself saying into the hollow of a third empty glass. He had sold himself in pieces throughout his life; one more fragment falling from the skeleton could leave only another small indentation somewhere. The disease of self-destruction had a slow progression.

"Thank you, Urb," she replied. A flash of youth surfed in her eyes. She knew they were joined in a kind of forced alchemy, both using alcohol like chemists to balance libidos, an ounce of this to counteract an urge for that, a compensating sip to bypass a desire for that.

Inevitably, they wound up in her apartment. He sought to delay the showdown, almost a necessity when she reappeared in the room half-stripped, her corset showing. It was one of the major turn-offs for him—a symbol of age.

"Do you need anything from me?" she asked honestly. "Any special postures or talk . . . ?"

"Don't be silly, Ruth. Just the sight of you is enough for any man."

"I can tell you like to go at things gradually. So let's have a drink." She stopped undressing, stopped rising and falling on her toes and heels to make her tits bounce and went for a high-necked bottle of brandy. Two pony glasses appeared almost magically from a table chest and were filled almost instantly.

"You're not going to get out of here alive," she laughed. "Relax before the tigress of Toledo devours you."

He coated a weak smile with strong brandy and it

seemed to strengthen under the lubrication. "We'll see who does what to whom," he said.

Somewhere in the thin, gray, no-man's-land separating night and day, in the tug-of-war between dark and dawn, he rose from his knees, flushed red with the imprint of her carpeting, withdrew his face from between her thighs and examined himself. He had been devoured, but not fatally. There was no recollection of a climax and not enough clues to be sure. But she was asleep and that filled him with a minor sense of victory. He cursed the cracking of his legs as he rose, imagining the sound to be much louder than it was, the way one imagines the sound of celery being masticated to carry throughout a room. His only fear of the moment was awakening her, with its threat of new demands upon him. But she was fully out, a thin stream of saliva trickling from the eastern delta of her lips, her nostrils dilated and looking from his vantage point like miniature tunnels overgrown with vegetation. There was nothing attractive about any woman asleep and drunk.

It was a sick way to live, he told himself again, as he had so often before under similar conditions with similar women. Out on the street in the ghostly pale of dawn, he looked vainly for a cab. Only then did he remember he was in Toledo, Ohio, and not New York, New York.

Noon was upon him like an enemy.

Elliot Ruskin had scheduled a one P.M. luncheon meeting of the GAF board in the Lakeland Hotel. Its purpose was to bring members up to date on the progress of their venture into big-time fund raising.

Urban shook himself loose from the clam of sheets he had entered only a few hours earlier. With his forefinger, he rubbed over the thick glue which seemed to cover his teeth. He did not dare to study himself in the mirror, going about the basic toiletry of society methodically, squirting his underarms with anti-perspirant, dousing his eyes with a guaranteed blood-shot-remover, rinsing his arid mouth with the contents of a plastic bottle of blue breath sweetner. He had misplaced his toothbrush, adding to his general agony, and the blade in his razor was more aggressive than helpful. His hair was combed by rote. He surveyed it finally with an oblique glance, deliberately keeping his face blurred. There was no point in any further nega-tive psyching of himself.

"Good to see you, Urban," Ruskin greeted him in the lobby. "You're looking well."

Urban smiled despite the pain. He had just proved one of his long-held theories: Few people really look at others, particularly in business relationships. "Thanks, Elliot," he said. "How do we stand?"

Ruskin joined his thumb and index finger in a circle, snapping the air with the makeshift ring. "So far, so good," he said. They went directly into the elevator, Elliot nudging him off at the second floor, then guiding him along a carpeted corridor to a set of double doors emblazoned: COMMODORE PERRY SUITE. He paused as his hand clutched one of the knobs. "Don't let any of them rattle you," he said evenly. "Let me pick it up if you're uncertain how to handle it."

Urban nodded. Forewarned is forearmed. Only it was a little late to arm himself. He had come to Toledo relatively free of anticipated problems—otherwise he would not have conducted himself as he had earlier the same day.

Ruskin clasped his shoulder, opened one of the doors and bowed Urban in ahead of him. The remainder of the board of directors was present, intact, and seated. They rose in unison as the two men entered. "Gentlemen," Elliot began pleasantly, "Mr. Giles is here with us again. Please be seated and let's proceed immediately with the matters at hand." Due to the varied business schedules of the members, in recognition of their volunteer membership, board matters were debated prior to lunch. The practice enabled everyone to hear the essentials and make his own decision on whether to remain for dining.

Elliot Ruskin, as president pro-tem since the death of the previous board chairman, called the meeting formally to order, waived reading of the minutes of the last session and called for committee reports.

The logistics committee chairman was first to detail progress. "We've secured a definite commitment from the management of the Paragon Theater for the use of all its facilities on September seventeenth——"

"Pardon me for interrupting, Julius," Urban said, "but I hope we also have them on the sixteenth to prepare the stage and telephone setups?"

"We do, Mr. Giles," he said, with some annoyance.

At the completion of the brief rundown, Ruskin called for the report of the personnel committee. "So far we have all the telephone operators from five hotels, plus several dozen volunteers from the phone company, to man the switchboards—which, incidentally, will be set up free of charge by the installers' union."

"We'll need at least a hundred girls, preferably fifty to a hundred more," Urban injected. The chairman smiled patiently. "We still have five months, Mr. Giles," he said.

And so it went through three more committees, most of them with overlapping membership since there were only thirteen men on the entire board. The key report, as far as Urban was concerned, came from the Entertainment Committee. It consisted of its selection of celebrities from the original list of availabilities he had submitted in his original presentation. He listened attentively as the chairman read off the roster, mentally calculating his own prospects for delivering on the choices.

Urban was cagey in his responses, avoiding any direct reaffirmation of any of them. "As I stressed before, gentlemen," he said, angling forward over the table, "the local amateur and professional contributions are as important, if not more so, than the stars who appear. My concern is not over your selections, but what is being done to date in the way of securing Toledo talent."

"It's a little early for that, Mr. Giles," said the small, bald man heading the committee.

"You're absolutely right," Urban said, spotting an escape hatch for himself. "I understand much of this is premature. I face much the same situation in negotiating with the names you've chosen. They're all busy people and September is a light year away. But let's all begin, let's all get under way to the maximum time factors allow. . . ."

Urban Giles had earned his B.S. degree without enrolling at any institution of higher learning.

The pledge committee reported contributions totaling seventy-eight thousand dollars already banked, a sum which bobbed heads and drew approving smiles around the long table. "Excellent," Ruskin said. "It's a good omen."

There were brief exchanges on other subjects and then a motion for adjournment. Before it could be seconded, the generally silent, crisply efficient man who sat across from Ruskin at the opposite reach of the table, Matthew Boylan, thrust himself upward. "May I have just a moment, Mr. President?" He held a sheet of paper in his hand and glanced downward at it as he spoke. "This is absolutely confidential among us here," he continued, "and I want Mr. Giles particularly to be assured of that. I assume it was addressed to me because I am affiliated with the publishing industry here. . . ." His eyes flicked toward Giles. "It comes from a Mr. Floyd Jasper, who is apparently a reporter for the New York *Register*. Are you familiar with him, Mr. Giles?"

Urban was not by nature a blusher, but he could feel the hot surge of blood to his face now. He had not pursued a career in politics, despite an inclination in that direction, because of his distaste for surprise challenges, for being disadvantaged by unexpected ploys, for being hit below the belt without warning. He had known from the beginning of his Toledo quest that Boylan did not like him and did not trust him. But this?

"I've had occasion to encounter him in the course of business in the past," Urban replied evenly. "Without kowing the contents of this letter to you, Mr. Boylan,

I would say unequivocally that I would discount much of what Jasper reports about anything."

Boylan smiled thinly. "The letter was addressed to me, Mr. Giles, but its salutation is to the entire board. Otherwise, I would not have introduced it at this meeting." He leaned over, extending the letter to Urban. "I think it only fair that you have an opportunity to read it first before it is circulated to the board."

Taken at face value, it was a damning document accusing Urban Giles Associates of excessive profiteering, shoddy performances, and calloused exploitation of unfortunate disease victims in not one, but *all* past telethon productions in New York. There were no details, only an invitation to the board to avail itself of the reporter's files if it so desired.

Urban read it hurriedly, as a defendant might read his notice of execution, and passed it to the member beside him. He was staring into a peacock's tail, all sorts of shining eyes surrounding him, but he remained silent as it made the round, one by one, on a chain of whispers and murmurs until it stopped finally at Elliot Ruskin. There, his command presence, seldom utilized, was summoned. He understood that arrogance in others is unpalatable even to the arrogant. But there were times when it became essential to activate it. The board was composed of a platoon of small dictators, most of whom wore their voluntary service to the Fund as another cluster on their civic achievement medals. Public service for private prestige, Elliot defined it. Because he understood that, he made a tower of himself and loomed over them.

"Gentlemen, I refuse to participate in any further

discussion or analysis of this absurd and unfounded character assassination of Mr. Urban Giles. Several of you here, three if I'm not mistaken, are attorneys at law. I'm certain you agree this letter is entirely without substance, is irrelevant and irresponsible, without any legal validity whatsoever. What one reporter for one newspaper, out of personal animosity or a need to fill newsprint or some other reason, has to say about a man whose record of financial success on behalf of multiple charities is unquestioned is entirely questionable to my mind. If this sort of innuendo is permitted to continue to its illogical conclusions, we might anticipate that Mr. Boylan or others of you will come foward one day with a Kinsey Report on Mr. Giles's life behind closed doors. . . ."

Urban let his eyes swim freely while his ears remained intent, marveling at the extemporaneous structuring of Ruskin's defense of him. He had missed his calling. He was a born trial lawyer.

"Before concluding and adjourning this meeting, gentlemen, I want to remind you of one very salient fact. We have a valid contract with Urban Giles Associates, all terms of which have thus far been met, and all future terms of which I'm certain will be equally upheld by all parties involved. On behalf of myself, my apologies to Mr. Giles for this unnecessary embarrassment. Thank you, gentlemen."

He sat down but rose immediately again, speaking above the flutter of papers being filed into briefcases. "We have a motion for adjournment still pending," he said. "Do we have a second?"

"I second the motion," Boylan said. He was not among those who remained for lunch.

Chapter Seven

Clarice met him at the airport, a noteworthy concession since the kids would be arriving home from school in her absence. She could have employed that excuse, as she had for weeks now, and he would have accepted it. It would have meant taking the bus into the Eastside Airlines Terminal and then another bus from the Port Authority Bus Terminal to Elmhill.

She could not have picked a more opportune time to begin a long overdue thaw in their relations. He was exhausted from the Toledo ordeal. To express his gratitude, in the strange manner of marital gratefulness, he did not press her to join him for his customary drinks before embarking for home.

"How are they?" He watched his breath fog the window as he spoke. There had not even been the usual debate over who would drive. He was too tired to be anything but a passenger.

"Maria's unhappy you didn't call her this time." She glanced over at him. "You look upset. Something wrong?"

"Yes and no."

Not having returned to the office as yet, she was cautious about expressing too much interest in his business operations. Still, they were an integral part of their lives, absolutely essential in the realm of economics. There was no way not to be concerned over them. "Did you see Ruth this trip?" she asked, changing the subject.

"Why?"

"You are upset. What's wrong?" Concern took form on her face, fluid lines winding and disbursed like tributaries at the delta of a river, little tangled branches of veins thwarting an ocean.

"Nothing I want to talk about now. Nothing important." He turned away and grew silent and she drove without questioning him further. Much as he would have fought and denied the image, she saw a Willie Loman quality about him as he climbed out of the car, gripped his bags and headed up the drive while she parked the car. She knew he hated the inroads of age, the ebbing of his youth, suddenly so apparent to her. She looked back, wanting to freeze life the way it had been once long ago. But there was no retrospective refrigeration, just as there was no warmth to remove the chill of her reality. Everything spoiled with age—love first, pity last.

"Are you all right?" she asked when she came through the kitchen. He had poured himself almost half a tumbler of whiskey and sat nursing it, his bags still on the floor beside him.

"Where are the kids?"

"They must be up the road. They've made friends with the Zimmerman kids."

"You let them out this late?"

"Six-fourteen. That's not late, Urb."

"Get them home."

She turned around and disappeared through the door. When they returned, his head was on the table. "Daddy's tired," Clarice said.

Maria kissed his forehead. "Good night, Daddy," she whispered. Ramon simply stood and looked and then all of them left him there and resumed their lives as though he was still hundreds of miles to the west of them.

Ruskin agreed it was best to suspend Urban's leap-frogging between New York and Toledo for the time being. Tentative plans now called for setting up an office in the Ohio city in mid-June. That would provide ample time to weave the fabric of a full production unit by September without leaving any loose ends.

He had been most understanding about everything, reaffirming a Giles theory that a percentage of the action worked wonders in cementing relations with almost anyone. Perhaps he should have approached Boylan as well. But he doubted it. True to an old Arabic adage—*the enemy of my enemy is my friend*—the encounter with Boylan had strengthened the relationship of Urban and Elliot. He reacted with much enthusiasm and encouragement to the news of their adoption of the children. In his dealings with the board, the Boylan revelation seemed to have increased his determination to push the entire project in Urban's behalf as much as for the Fund. There was, of course, the incidental matter of his own participation, too.

"I've got a summer place at Lake St. Clair," he informed him upon learning of the adoptions. "I want you and Clarice and the children to enjoy it while you're setting up in town." The offer included a cabin cruiser and guest membership in a posh Grosse Pointe yacht club. It was a perfect solution to the summer vacation problem for the Giles clan, now doubled in size. He accepted it gratefully.

With one half of one year of his remaining life now seemingly organized, at least tentatively, he decided to stay out of Manhattan for a week and remain at home. It was high time he became more than superficially acquainted with the new members of his family. The coincidence of a spring vacation from school removed his last hesitation.

A long night's rest renewed him, lubricating his joints, smoothing out his skin, painting color back into his lips and cheeks, removing the red mesh from his eyes. He was pleased by his appearance in the bathroom mirror for the first time in weeks—pleased also by the limber erection stirring in his pajamas until he freed it over the bowl, releasing the night's backup of urine. It was also a first time, not in weeks but months.

Refreshed, even exhilarated by the mild pain of the after-shave lotion, he set about constructing a day with Maria and Ramon. It was impossible for him to simply enter a day and let it unfold, even a day of alleged leisure. Planning separated clods from achievers. That applied to vacations as well as vocations.

"After breakfast, we'll drive over to Interstate Park, take a nice hike in the woods, then lunch at Bear Mountain Inn. After that, we'll visit the military academy at West Point, bat a few balls around for a while,

then look for a nice little country place to have dinner—"

"Sounds like an all-eating day," Clarice said. He
knew she meant all-spending and ignored her comment.

"How about it, Maria?" The girl's eyes skated about
the room, flashing like blades over ice. She nodded her
head in happy agreement.

"Ramon? What's your verdict?"

His smile shone fishbone white over the kitchen
table. They were a pleasure to proposition, Urban
thought to himself. On his best business days his ideas
never met with such enthusiasm. He had succeeded up
to now in keeping his thoughts moving, circling, avoiding any concentration on Maria. Perhaps that was due
to meeting the hook-ended, question-mark glances of
Clarice every time his eyes tarried on the girl. But he
gave her no real indication of what thoughts now
limned his mind. Both of them had adopted a code of
silence regarding any prior motivations from the moment the adoptions became certain. Neither knew any
longer what remained of the past within the other.

Without a meeting or vote, simply by spontaneity, it
had been decided that Maria was to call her new
parents Mommy and Daddy, while Ramon would address them as Urb and Clare.

"Can I sit up front with Urb?" Ramon asked while
Urban went for the car.

"If you like," Clarice said. He dug the toe of his
shoe into the soft turf, a move she had already learned
to recognize as an indication of pleasure or satisfaction.

"Okay," he said.

"You mean 'thank you,' " she corrected.

He looked up, puzzled.

"Polite people always say thank you when someone does something nice for them," she explained.

"Thank you," he said with some hesitance.

Urban drew up to them, still marveling at the good condition of his spirits. All things considered, he did not have an excess of good things to celebrate. Yet here he was, his inner tempo unaccountably accelerated, buoyant, even reckless. All days were not the same, no matter how similar their beginnings.

"Ramon wants to sit up front with you," Clarice said.

"Good. I need a copilot."

"Boys have all the fun," Maria said.

Urban threw a look at her over his shoulder, ensnaring his wife in the broad loop of it. "You'll get your turn, Maria," he said.

The park was almost empty. It was easy to understand why after they tested the ground beyond the tarred parking area. The thin spring sun had scarcely filtered through the tall trees, leaving the earth still matted and soggy, damp leaves and underbrush making a winter-logged carpet of the ground.

Only Maria seemed game to venture into the dank forest with Urban. Ramon preferred to study the engine components under the hood of the car, a subject which increasingly fascinated him. As for Clarice, she was the original timid soul in matters of exploring the unknown, even when it was within the bounds of a government park. And so it was just the two of them, foster father and daughter, who fulfilled the first part of his game plan for the day. They disappeared hand-in-hand into a thick stand of oaks.

"Be careful!" Clarice shouted after them. There were dangers unrelated to flora and fauna lurking beyond her vision. Some of them, she concluded with resignation, were inevitable. It would do no good to worry.

In the forest, Maria insisted on swinging from a low-hanging branch at the edge of a clearing. "Boost me up, Daddy," she said.

He reached under her jacket to clutch her waist, his fingers spidering momentarily upward as though lost, touching her firm breasts swiftly, delicately, hungrily, before sliding downward again to grasp the supple middle of her. He was forced to hesitate briefly, weakened by the surge of lust gripping him, then tightened his arms and lifted her past his face.

"Higher," she directed.

His hands became a ratchet lift, inching her upward until his thumbs dug into the soft flesh of her buttocks, almost separating them above his face. The view above him, through the thin gauze of her panties, flung him hard against the restraining wall of his slacks.

"There," she said finally when he thought he could hold her no longer, when the lower demands upon him, the counter tensions, seemed certain to usurp all his energy and strength. She swung free of him, lightly, to and fro, her body becoming a willow in the wind.

A decision had to be made immediately. The swelling had become almost painful in its urgency. He turned his back to her and dug into himself, removing the swollen penis, milking it rapidly, his fist slamming from the hairy base of it to the saturn rings about its crown. He had to relieve himself or go crazy. Or rush his own ultimate plans. But this was not the time nor the place. He retained just enough control of himself to realize that.

"What're you doing, Daddy?" She was suddenly beside him, witnessing the frantic shimmy of his hand, a strange, special brightness to her eyes.

Her voice triggered him, his body recoiling from the explosion of compressed libido, thick vanilla pearls spilling from the tip of him, strung on a transparent necklace, gathering like spent silver at his feet. He could not speak immediately, sucking in the damp air instead, watching it escape from him in small clouds. When his chest had quieted, he turned and angled himself away from her, wiping the tapioca from his cock with a handkerchief fished from his back pocket. His eyes gleamed, whether from fright or delight she could not tell, but she looked away and said nothing.

"Daddy was sick for a minute," he said. "Don't tell Mommy about it, though. She'll just worry." His ability to read people, an achievement in which he prided himself, did not extend to children. Yet strangely, he was not remorseful or even frightened. Instead, he felt a lingering passion circulating through him, warm and promising.

"You heard me, Maria? You're not to tell Mommy."

She nodded. He took her hand and they sliced back into the curtain of trees, toward the car.

"Mommy, I swung from a big, high tree," she reported at the lot.

Urban nosed the car out of the forest, onto a secondary highway, and headed for Bear Mountain. Nothing could go wrong with a day that began as this one had.

It was difficult to be clinical about sex when one's own passions were involved. But that night, lying alone on the quilted bed, his head shored up by three pillows, he attempted to analyze his position in the matter of Maria.

All right, technically she was his daughter. He preferred not to think of her with a title, only a name. But if he must, then he did have the consolation of knowing she was not his biological daughter. He had only contempt for fathers who committed incest and the thought of himself in such a category was revolting to him. Stigma removed, then there was the matter of her youth. Well, he was assured she was into puberty. He had seen the junior tampons in the medicine cabinet— they were certainly not intended to fill Clarice's cavern. And there were traces of stains in her discarded panties, further confirming she had begun menstruating. Unwillingly, likely because of its sanguinary nature, he could not help recalling a cold, barroom adage he had once overheard. "If they're old enough to bleed, they're old enough to butcher," it stated. He chased it from his thoughts, returning himself to more pleasant contemplations. Between his legs, the simmering of his mental exercises began working its special magic, stirring the folds of his pajamas. In many parts of the world, his mind continued—India, Pakistan, Guatemala, to name a few—she was of marriageable age, a potential mother. The image of her crossed his mind now and he allowed himself to concentrate upon it, fresh impressions intact, as though he were at an art exhibit and she was a painting on display. Rapidly, the illusion transformed into the previous morning, solidifying him with the taunt of its unrealized dream.

He got up and pulled on his robe, making certain most of him was disguised by the overlap of its folds, and went into Maria's room. She lay sandwiched between the sheets, her lovely face framed by its even fall of black hair, her mouth slightly parted, her breath soft and sweet in the stillness. He looked at her a long time before bending over and kissing her lips.

Clarice awaited him in his room. His first reaction was startled, that of a night marauder flushed by a hunter. But then he saw no visible traces of reproach on her face, restoring his equanimity. She moved against him in the shadowed light, meeting the still imposing thrust of his erection as though she had been anticipating it.

There were no preliminaries because there was no necessity. At this hour, neither questioned the other's source of arousal, moving only to expedite and accommodate it. Perhaps it had been a special day for her, too. He did not really care. Here was an opportunity, unexpected at that, to plunge his frustration deep into his wife and calm himself for sleep.

"Fuck me," she said. Her voice came from somewhere in the tangle of their bodies, fallen upon the bed with no concern for order or direction. She never used obscenities except in sexual situations and the sound of her spitting the word into the night jacked him upward another notch. He drove into her, pounding his stake into the quivering crotch of her, his lust now full and domineering, ripping at the slippery delta of her legs. They climaxed together, with no verbal warnings necessary for timing, lying there until they could renew themselves, escaping briefly, separately, to wash themselves. They renewed at opposite poles, attracted by some unwritten law of physical magnetism, lips to cunt, cock to lips, faces slick with the glycerine of desire.

Minutes like hours and hours like minutes, they lay sucking at one another as though the breath of life was available only through the other, lost for the moments in the illusions and delusions of their lives, playing the scenes of their fantasies against the sterile backdrop of a room she had emptied and now would never fully refill.

He saw Maria first, microscopic seconds before Clarice caught the signal relayed by his nervous system. She stood silhouetted in the doorway, slivers of light glinting from the white silk of her eyes. Clarice could not fully focus her, the whole interior of herself suddenly drawn into a single fistful of guts and slammed against a wall, all the lubricants of her body running and then freezing.

"Maria," she gasped. "What are you doing up?"

"I'm thirsty," the girl said.

Initiative was the key word for Urban's programming the following morning. It was no longer necessary to circumvent Clarice. By reawakening the dormant animal in her nature, he had won her to his side more completely than all his persuasive salesmanship had accomplished in the past. She had begun, ever so slightly, to accept the duality possible in their unique situation—even though she was not yet ready or willing to be a participant.

"Be gentle with her," was her repeated warning, her only admonition.

A new liberalism was apparent to her immediately. He began fondling the girl openly, under the guise of playing, enlisting Ramon in a hybrid game of football-basketball-soccer on the lawn, the game's only object being to provide Urban with opportunities to feel her body. If the boy caught any of the nuances, any of the furtive clutches and grabs and grasps caressing his sister, he gave no indication, obeying the makeshift rules with boyish diligence, celebrating each of his scoring efforts as though it really mattered.

They went inside in the late afternoon for Cokes and cookies. Rum was added to Urban's drink to make it palatable, of course. He began placing unusual stress on their mutual needs for baths after the rousing game, making his next move as obvious to Clarice as if it were outlined in neon.

"Ray, you go first because you were top scorer. Then Maria, then me." The victor angle was good basic psychology. Ramon gulped down the remainder of his drink to speed up his claim on first prize.

When he had left the room, the sound of the shower following like rain drumming against a distant wall, Urban raked his fingers through Maria's hair. "So how did my little girl sleep last night?" he asked.

"Yes, Maria, I meant to ask you. How did you sleep after getting up in the middle of the night?" Clarice injected.

A little learning might well be a dangerous thing, but it can also be a powerful stimulant to learn more. Maria had inhaled only a tiny essence of a mysterious potion there at the edge of their bedroom. The desire for more, for a full taste of it, had stirred in her the remainder of the night, touching her body where she hardly dared touch herself, holding off sleep with its elusive promise of further intrigue. Her eyes reacted to the questions with the look of the moon on dark water, shimmering, twinkling, but giving no glimpse of what currents flowed beneath the surface. She played her long lashes like teasing veils over them, making her now more seductive than seducible. It aroused him instantly and he turned away to delay himself.

"I was tired," she replied finally.

"Better go to bed a little earlier tonight," Clarice advised. "Especially after all that running around to-day."

Ramon appeared in his pajama bottoms, his back still jeweled with drops of water. "Bring me a towel," she instructed him. "Boys just never dry their backs or behind their ears."

Maria giggled at the accusation and the mock disgust in her mother's voice. She watched fascinated as Clarice rubbed the thick pile over the breadth of his back, massaging the strong shoulders as she bunched the towel around his neck, stroking the valleys behind his ears aggressively, climaxing the drying exercise with a vigorous stropping of his head and hair. "Now, get me a comb," she said.

He was reluctant to permit her to part his hair, but she overrode him, separating it into neat black sheets, then combing it back along the sides and over the top until he resembled a handsome mannequin perfectly coiffed. The decorating of him gave her unusual satisfaction, a unique kind of pleasure she had not experienced before. She clasped his shoulders when she was finished, pressing her lips into one of them until she could feel its texture.

"There," she said, releasing him, "you look like a Greek god."

He stepped back, head bent bashfully, embarrassed because his audience included Maria.

"Okay, little Maria," Urban said, "you're next." He rose with her, steering her toward the bathroom. "Let me check to make sure Ray hasn't flooded the place."

"I didn't," Ramon protested.

"Okay, Ray. Relax." A tremor of anxiety rippled his flesh as he entered the room with her. He busied himself with a brush, pretending to be scrubbing the tub to prepare it for her entry. "Want me to fix the water for you, honey?"

"Yes. I always get it too hot."

He dialed the two control knobs, hot and cold, fingering the loud torrent pouring from between them. "How's this?" He nodded toward the water gathering over the tub bottom.

She bent across him as he sat on the edge of the tub, her midriff touching the hard thrust of him. For a fleeting second, her eyes skipped to his. Then she inserted her open hand into the gush of water, letting it fall into her palm as though balancing and weighing it. "That's just right," she said.

"I like it this way, too. Why don't we take a bath together, just for fun?"

She looked at him fully now, shyly, but with surprising surety. "Okay," she said.

He moved carefully within his clothes, afraid the slightest contact, even with his own garments, would trigger an ejaculation. The excitement was so intense he was forced to look away from her for a moment, missing a sequence of the drama of her disrobing. When he returned his gaze, only her panties remained like a dainty lilac veil over the last mystery of her. He drank in the lovely hills rising above them, the nipples like young strawberries, and then skinned the last piece of apparel from her.

She stood motionless as he proceeded, only her eyes expanding with each fresh contact, allowing herself to be explored the way a dog permits another to inhale and examine and touch her, hardly participating beyond making a warm and willing statue of her body.

He stopped momentarily to rip off his own clothes, his prick falling like a drawbridge from his pants, spanning the tile moat between them. The water had risen high in the tub. He leaned back awkwardly to turn off the flow, unwilling to break the flesh contact with her for such a pedestrian task. Reverently, he lifted her face by its chin, the luster of it almost tactile, fingering his own lips to indicate silence when the water's sound cover had ended.

Where to begin with such a delicacy before him? She awaited his advance and direction, incapable of understanding his hesitancy at the realization of a fantasy, this tangible object replacing a mental portrait, a dream distilled from vapors and now turned into a chemical reality.

She fixed her eyes on the massive cylinder of flesh daubing her skin with its gleaming mucilage, at the balls clinging tightly to the base of it, hard and haired like small coconuts. She had seen Ramon, as she had seen other boys, but none with the size and solidity and gut-red coloring of the cock now seething to enter her.

How many times he had imagined and analyzed his procedure in a situation such as he was now in! How little his theories now appealed to him. He much preferred the random sampling in which he was indulging, splitting the moist lips of her vagina with his thumb and forefinger as though it were zippered, tiptoeing his fingers through the lacy fringe of virgin forest bordering it, sucking the tender fruit of her bosom, cupping the melons of her buttocks, intoxicated by the rise of his own juices now nearing flood stage at the dam of his cock.

With labored restraint, he moved himself into position to enter her, lowering her to his lap slowly, gently, his thumbs in the crevice behind her, parting the cheeks as though separating a ripe peach from its stone. She settled her lips instinctively, like a sheath, over the ruby crest, testing her capacity against the intruder, lubricating it and being lubricated in return. "It's my pussy," she whispered in his ear, proud of its ability to receive so much of him.

Her words tripped the precarious balance within him. Frantically, he pulled out of her, aiming the sequence of shots toward her abdomen, decorating it as though he was icing a cake. She had seen the same silver-gray spurting from him in the forest. What she had only remotely understood then was much clearer now.

He did not get into the tub with her as they had planned only moments before. There would be many more times to innovate and elaborate. Instead, he bent down and kissed her pussy fully. "Take your bath now, darling," he said.

She reached out and petted his cock. "You're not sick anymore, are you?" Before he could answer, she had slipped gracefully into the small lake of bath water and submerged.

In his room, he pulled on his bathrobe and prepared to reenter the family circle. The sound of the television set echoed down the hall. He knew he had not been missed. Not by Ramon. All of a sudden, the role of father had become the most fascinating aspect of his life.

Chapter Eight

It was sometimes a mosaic, orderly but multicolored, more often a jigsaw puzzle, incomplete, with pieces missing. That was life for Urban Giles, with the necessity to survive intruding upon his pleasures, just as it did for lesser men. And better men. It left him with a vague envy of the wealthy and their opportunities to circulate without the shackles of economics.

But within it all, he had his gates and tunnels, his shortcuts and broken fences, and he utilized them with the skill of a burglar when necessary. He was capable of closing off portions of his mind like unoccupied rooms of a busy hotel, traveling its corridors without entering its units. He was intelligent and perceptive, but he was also weak and foolish. The deficits were currently outweighing the strengths.

Ruskin had left three messages during his week of home-vacationing. Instead of answering them immediately, he merely rummaged about his desk, sorted his mail and left. Outside, he wandered first into a bar in which he was not known, drank three quick double shots, then plunged into a downstairs bowling alley just off Broadway. There, amidst the sharp clatter of falling pins, he drank two bottles of beer and departed abruptly, climbing upward as though escaping some underground terror. Back in the gray air, he turned left and strode determinedly down Broadway, convincing himself of an urgent destination.

The synthetic garden of lights on Forty-second Street swung him westward. He glanced into the bare pornography parlors, their cheap magazines slotted against the walls, stopping finally at the remnants of an arcade promising "Fun-Games-Entertainment." His head was swimming by now, his mind humming. Even his libido had vacated him for a time, freeing him of the haunting stimuli of Elmhill, leaving him to observe and float and reflect in a world spun and looped instead of sharp-edged and demanding. He laughed at the remembrance of a recent psychological study which had determined that men of his age thought of sex once an hour. Until the advent of his current looseness, he believed once a minute was a more accurate figure.

Positioning himself over a pinball machine, he inserted a quarter, conducting his own ad-libbed research on humanity as he played. It was against his work ethic not to be involved in something constructive at all times. What better justification for his presence in a cheap arcade in midafternoon than the conducting of a psychological survey? He was lost there among the empty faces, listening to the losers' serenade of pinging circuit bumpers and shrill bell alarms. It was good to be away from everything, he told himself. His eyes toured his own hands as he embraced the machine in a posture of anal intercourse, seeing with sudden clarity the blue veins piled there, grasping upward along his arms like lines on a blueprint, highways on a map leading to the source of his life. Now it was no longer good to be away. The reminder of his own fading mortality brought a steep depression and he looked away, outward at the young addicts hunched over the psychedelic displays of their machines, squandering bits of money as they did their lives. They lived here, on this street, their ping-pong lives colored by the flicks and flashes of studded lights, as barren as the cold neon probing their faces, moving like animals in a mazda jungle. They got high and then stoned and then came to the arcade and played pinball machines, imagining a rhythm to them, combining lights and sounds into a cheap fantasy, their bodies swaying, accentuating, pushing, pulling, loosening to the tempo of flashing electricity. He had to admit it was satisfying in its brevity, all bases seeming to be touched while spending only a small portion of the day's total emotions. But there was also a sickening artificiality to it all, a purgatory quality, and he moved to rid himself of it, rushing through the spindly tawdriness of the place, bells ringing and taunting from every corner, lights oning and offing, its inhabitants staring at him with glazed eyes, fruited on the looms of their own skeletal fantasies, warped by the necessity to win, even if only over themselves—unwilling to acknowledge their losses, hollow champions, victors over nothing, undeclared, unrecognized, unwanted and alone in the shallow, petty, temporary triumphs over a machine.

He could not turn himself off as he fled through the door and merged with the passing crowd, no longer carefree, having glimpsed too much of himself in the faces of others, having descended a step into hell and unwillingly found a place for himself. He moved swiftly now through the layers of people, back toward Times Square, as though speed and distance would rid him of the taint of his experience.

The Algonquin Hotel loomed before him on Forty-fourth Street and he hurried up its steps into the little bar to the right of the entrance. Now he would be all right, harbored in the citadel of past literary giants, of the Round Table, of gentility and success and dreams realized instead of shattered.

The first martini went down like beer, in a single, prolonged swallow, the slash of lemon peel almost clogging his throat.

"Tough day?" the bartender asked with practiced concern.

"Rough," he said, pushing the glass toward him for refilling. Careful, Urbie, old boy, he warned himself. You're getting drunk and they don't serve drunks in the Algonquin. He let the second one sit before him for what seemed a decent interval, then lifted it quickly to his lips. What was wrong, what was going wrong with him? He refused to consider it a legitimate question and returned to other, less troubling thoughts.

Somewhere along in the interlude, perhaps three

martinis later, when the walking nightmare had disappeared, he struggled to his feet and collected his
thoughts. They were not pleasant and he could not
account for their presence.

The day had been a total loss.

Clarice Giles saw the deterioration in him more
graphically as she sought strength from him. It had
always been a precarious existence, a roller-coaster life
of ups and downs; slow climbs and speedy descents. But
now there was more than just the two of them and she
was frankly alarmed.

She had made a reluctant decision to return to Urban Giles Associates in her old role as senior partner.
Somehow she had not yet been able to tell him of her
plan, hoping vaguely it would not become necessary.
But there was no longer any real alternative. It was
either that or the collapse of the firm.

The children were old enough to be alone for several hours after school until they returned from the city.
There would be no need to permit a stranger to enter
their secret world, a prospect both of them regarded as
not merely impractical but impossible.

Arriving at the decision had the unexpected side
effect of buoying her spirits, making her able once
more to entertain hopes and thoughts and illusions she
had long crowded into a closet of her mind. The children noticed the change in her almost immediately.

"You act just like a little girl, Mommy," Marie observed not long after. "How come?"

"I'm happy," she explained. "I'm happy you and
Ramon are here. I'm happy I'm going to help Daddy
again."

"Will you sleep with him then?"

Clarice poked her lightly. "Do you think I should?"

"Yes."

"Maybe we'll all sleep together," she said with a laugh. "How would you like that, Ramon?"

He grinned at the suggestion. "No bed is big enough," he said.

In this state of bubbly suspension, she had made her first discovery of his official emergence into manhood. It excited her beyond what she had admitted, could or would admit to anyone. Her attitude toward Urban's fantasy projections had always been one of tolerant neutrality. She went along with them to aid his sexual pleasure, emphasizing later that her agreement had only been in his behalf, to assist his own fulfillment. But now she had begun to realize that was not entirely accurate. Her realization had come the moment she first saw Ramon step lithe and naked from the shower, his young genitalia a lovely cluster at the apex of his legs. After that, when Urban accomplished his long-whispered dream in the same setting, her imagination had begun dramatizing the scene repeatedly within her, stirring the twilight moments just before she succumbed to sleep. She had not mentioned any of it to him. His business conduct had been altogether too distressing to permit her easy expression of inner thoughts, if indeed she could ever reveal them. Still, they had remained there, a permanent part now of the chemistry of her and she could not deny it to herself.

Ramon took care of his own room—making his bed, emptying the wastebasket, hanging up his clothes, dusting, washing his window. The only routine duty left to

Clarice was laundering, then stocking his drawers with the clean clothes. It was there, in the second drawer of the dresser, that she made her discovery. He had semi-hidden several of his socks under a pile of handkerchiefs, rolling them carefully to resemble the others in front of them. When she touched them, out of curiosity because they had not appeared in the laundry for weeks, she knew immediately the reason. They were stiff, matted along the arches, a distinctive, thready white substance dried and crusted midway along them. She had smiled at the nostalgia of it. Her own brother had done the same thing—except that he had been severely reprimanded for it. She would say nothing. In fact, in the midst of her remembrance of it, she had become suddenly aroused, picturing him masturbating into them, his tender young cock alert and rigid, the sock fitted over it like a condom, his fresh virility splashing into them. She had taken his hairbrush then, clutching its bristles, and inserted the smooth handle into herself, revolving herself as she clasped the balls of his impregnated socks to her breast. It had been a rich moment for her, one she had been unable to forget since. Whenever she saw him now, the picture returned. It inspired a quiet determination to come upon him in reenactment of it.

Seek and ye shall find, the Bible promised, and so she did on an afternoon when Maria had gone to the Zimmermans for a birthday party honoring their daughter, her classmate Diane. Ramon had gone upstairs immediately, a long silence following his arrival there. Clarice turned the radio on in the kitchen, creating the illusion of supper preparations, and crept up the carpeted stairs, carefully avoiding several spots where the old wood creaked.

Her ruse had worked. His door remained partially opened. And sure enough, he was there playing with himself, milking the tip of his penis between his thumb and index finger, leaning back to exult in the power and glory of his new masculinity, a sock clutched in his other hand ready to be hooded over the dragon the moment it chose to spit.

She adored the scene. Voyeuristically, it was satisfying within itself. But she was unwilling to risk the possibility of another chance to introduce herself to him as he had never yet known her. Now or never, she decided. Swiftly, silently, she stripped herself, freeing her hard-nippled tits, stroking the coiffure of her vagina, examining herself in a quick downward sweep of her eyes, readying herself for the ecstasy of an unexpected meeting with a forbidden lover. She understood now what Urban had been advocating all along.

Entering softly, seeking not to startle him, she spoke with a whispered huskiness. "What are you doing, Ramon?"

Her precaution was totally ineffective. Any boy caught in the act of jacking off is instinctively startled. Ramon recoiled at the sight of her, hardly noticing her nudity, his hand dropping from his cock as though it had caught fire. She did not wait for a further reaction to set in, embracing him immediately, all but surrounding him, reaching easily, surely, for the erection, stroking it to maintain it, petting it, reveling in its sleek firmness. The urge to devour it was strong and persistent, but here, strangely, her maternal balance intercepted the weight of her desire. She wanted to teach him gradually, naturally, saving the epicurean extras for later in his education, limiting her own appetite for the sake of future feasts. But she did permit herself to feed her eyes with the sight of it, peeling back its foreskin gently, like leaves around a tender shoot. The head of it blushed with sensitivity at her touch, a small, glistening fountain emerging from it and silvering its sides. She took his hands and placed them on her breasts, lifting them on the tray of her own hands until the nipples rose to his face. "Kiss them for me, Ramon, will you please?"

He did as he was asked, embellishing his kisses with an instinctive twist of his tongue, sending a jolt of pleasure through her. "You're going to be some lover, darling," she said with lips wide. He had not spoken at all since her entry into the room, too occupied with the difficult transition, the swift leap from imagination to reality, from masturbation to mammary glands, from mother to lover, from boy to man.

She led him to his bed and fell there, onto her back, legs opening in invitation. No instructions were necessary. She verbalized now for reference and pleasure. "Do you know what this is called?" He drew himself in and out of her with the speed of youth, an exciting change from the slowness of Urban's recent performances.

"Fucking," he said.

As he said it, she felt the fierce firepower of his age awash within her, splashing the heated walls of her, silver white bullets disintegrating against their target. It was all she needed to set her body into convulsions, a sequence of climaxes multiplying down the corridor of her interior like liquid echoes, reducing questions and answers to mere moans, too deeply felt to find form in words.

He was able to repeat himself immediately, displaying a new eagerness now that all barriers were down. She welcomed him again, the fever returning with the sharp intrusion of his young cock, the thought of future encounters giving added beauty to this premiere performance.

For once it was a good thing Urban arrived home with too much to drink. This way he could not recognize her own intoxication. The only difference was she had not been drinking.

Chapter Nine

Winter and its sullenness, spring and its caprices, fled into the warm arms of June with no major business abrasions. Urban had reestablished his old relationship with Steven Lederer. As assistant to the president of Whitcomb & Wiley, he had access to some of the most important names in show business. The agency ranked number one in media sponsorship.

Lederer would be pieced off, as he had been in the past, thereby guaranteeing a full retinue of celebrities for the Toledo telecast. Very few names were so securely established, so loftily elevated, that they could afford to ignore a summons from the people who con-

trolled millions in advertising dollars and the shows
that went with their expenditure. There was a slight
technicality which troubled both of them—the matter
of the telethon being in Toledo and not in New York—
but their own reservations were dismissed over multiple
martinis. They were all optimism by the end of the
afternoon. Urban was further cheered the same day
with the arrival of another advance-expenses check for
fifteen thousand dollars. It immediately expedited the
move of the Giles clan to Elliot Ruskin's summer place
on Lake St. Clair.

The relationship of Urban and Clarice had certainly
been clarified, if not vastly improved, with her admission of participation in his original adoption plan. She
had even discussed and approved his latest variation—
summer sleeping arrangements. Maria was to sleep with
him, Ramon with Clarice. They would no longer be
subject to invasions of classmates or neighbors as they
were at Elmhill, where a semblance of separation was
essential. Summer houses did not have clearly identifiable rooms. There were just bedrooms and living rooms,
kitchens and bathrooms, all alike for children and
adults. The prospect of the new setup was as pleasurable to them as that of their first prolonged vacation in
years.

Ruth Fuller was everywhere about the place from
the beginning. The implication was that she had be-
stowed the blessing of summer shelter upon them. At
least, that was Clarice's interpretation of her constant
intrusion. With almost stereotyped middle-age childless-
ness, she smothered kisses upon the children without
concern for their reaction. It was as though her barrenness gave her special privileges of overindulgence.

Clarice could not deny a certain mild jealousy over her seeming fascination with Ramon. Her excessive attentions to Urban disturbed her far, far less.

The lake itself was lovely and placid. The water, due to its shallowness, was a unique green—a billiard table lined with moss and sparkled with emeralds. They studied it together at their first opportunity and decided it was worth whatever visitation disadvantages Ruth might impose. A certain temporary serenity had come over their own relationship, even resulting infrequently in quite elaborate and satisfying relations between them. He attributed it to the fantasy factor for lack of a better explanation. It was true that he was really fucking Maria, or another young girl, even as he entered and exited Clarice. But then, all men did that. And all women. Sexual success involved aspiration, he reasoned, not conquest itself. There were many days now when he thought of going beyond Maria to achieve new heights of resolution. Was there no final summit? He decided, with some sadness, there was not. And that realization calmed him, along with the aid of gin and vermouth, when his libido became unduly restless.

The car culture of the Detroit area began immediately to permeate their lives there. The people about them were mostly car people—executives to be sure—totally car-oriented. There was incessant car talk, car love, car worship, car status, car pasts and car futures, as though the world had begun in their century with the invention of the automobile, as though it would end if and when the automobile industry ended. What was good for General Motors was pluperfect good for Grosse Pointe.

Urban moved easily among pretenders, but things became more difficult for him in the realm of real achievers, authentic blue blood and Blue Book membership. They accepted him with the characteristic grace and manners of their breeding. But it was surface acceptance, not extending much beyond the cocktail lounge and dining room of the yacht club. There were no invitations to their homes, only an occasional bid to board their boats.

His life had always been populated with Hollywood name people; euphonious, alliterative names manufactured to be both visually and verbally pleasing. No one assumed them to be the same names as existed on their birth certificates, no one knew what unflattering nicknames they might have endured in childhood. But these were people with names beyond the ken of most press-agent imaginations. In one evening aboard the cruiser of a local banker, he met men named Ashley Worthington, Brooks Claiborne, Reginald Hayworth, Elton Stone and Stewart Richter. It pleased him in an oblique way that his own name stood the test of such exclusivity even if his credentials did not.

"Giles?" the man named Claiborne asked without being inquisitive—a rare facility also possessed in abundance by these people. "Giles of Boston, by chance?"

"I'm from New York," Urban volunteered. "Urban Giles Associates."

"Oh, yes," Claiborne said politely. "Investment banking."

"No," Urban replied. "Entertainment productions, primarily telethons."

The man fled from him as soon as he could discreetly maneuver himself away. In the autumn of the twentieth century, the aristocracy still looked upon show business as a subsidiary of the oldest profession. Or vice versa. He wondered later, when the martinis had begun to take hold, if any of them ever deigned to view the lowly tube. It was a good thing for his profession that the upper crust of the nation was concentrated in a very slender layer.

Ruth had brought him to the shipboard party, with Clarice's permission. It was, after all, primarily a business matter since several potentially major donors were present. The men in question proved wary and elusive throughout the long afternoon, departing finally without any real commitment to contribute.

They went to a motel after that, ostensibly for a drink at the bar, yet both hesitated and then stopped at the lobby registration desk. "We need a passport to the lounge," he had joked, feigning enthusiasm over the inevitable. It turned out to be an uninspired performance, at least on his part. Ruth Fuller was too much a lady, or perhaps too much an egotist, to force a man through an encore. She suggested instead they return to the bar for a nightcap, promising to drive him back to the summer house.

Time expanded and contracted for several hours, floating freely, suspended, whirling like a compass at the poles, clicking like a shutter, taking time exposures and snapshots, up tight and then distant, important and meaningless, strung with sentences and then emptying into silence until they were surrounded by murmurs of people taking form in the darkness, rising about them in a newly planted garden, stalks and clusters huddled over tiny tables, sequins and diamonds twinkling like fireflies from the limbs of some, red erasers glowing on the ends of white pencil cigarettes, the black-jacketed waiters transformed into long-legged girls in mini-aprons.

Gradually it all came into focus, a dawn of subdued lighting rising about the edges, revealing a low-ceilinged, blue-and-white polka-dotted world where only a dim cocktail lounge existed earlier. They had survived the late afternoon and early evening only to be enlisted in the audience of a nightclub, its featured entertainment heralded now by the rustling of everyone and everything, like leaves stirring in the warning wind of an approaching summer storm.

"Should we stay?" he asked her.

She looked up, eyes heavy-lidded and Draculan in the corkscrew twists of light tapering upward from a table candle. "Been hare thish long," she said slurringly, "lesh she what'sh going on."

He was beyond caring one way or the other, beckoning a waitress to the table. "Better make it gin and tonic this time," he said distinctly. His martini level had been attained and exceeded long before and still his voice emerged even and clear. The girl glanced questioningly at Ruth but said nothing. They were both fashionably dressed, however unfashionable their condition, and that seemed to qualify them to remain.

After so many hours, little was left to discuss. And there was even less inclination to attempt discussing it. A trio moved onto the small stage, mechanically launching into a medley of standards, a few couples rising to feign dancing on the tiny floor, inserting themselves into one another, indulging their separate and mutual exhibitionism, entertaining brief fantasies of stardom before an audience, under the lights. It amused him how people aspired to recognition as performers. He looked about the room, watching the way they gathered in tabled coveys, sucking at the synthetic sun of the stage, imagining an incandescence of their own in the play of pin spotlights, applauding wildly out of proportion to the worth of the main attraction when he finally swiveled his way onstage, toying with a hand mike, all but performing fellatio upon it, faking modesty in little head bows, uncaging his ego in dramatic flourishes the audience mistook for talent. Urban would not even use him on a telethon, he decided, unless of course he was caught with dead time around four or five in the morning, the graveyard hours for around-the-clock telecasting.

"Let's go," he said when the man finally completed his loud but dreary performance.

They had tested their legs earlier in journeys to the rest rooms. She had been gone for more than half an hour, which passed like minutes to him. He could lose himself within himself at times. In a sea of liquor such as he had consumed this day, he could swim aimlessly for hours.

Ruth rose easily and accurately, the result of her revival technique in the powder room. It involved much facial water splashing, eye lotioning and application of new makeup. The process was not unique, but it worked, even knocking the slush sounds from her speech. Urban was not nearly so steady, lurching toward the lobby exit, brushing against several table squatters en route, flinging apologies over his shoulder as he wandered, finally righting himself against a pillar.

"Want to lie down in the room for a while?" she asked.

"What time is it?"

She threw a searching look about the lobby, finally locating a clock behind the registration desk. "Oh, God," she said. "It's past ten-thirty."

He was instantly erect. "Got to get back. Board meeting tomorrow."

"I know."

"Jesus! How did we get so loaded?"

"Don't worry. I can drive."

"Jesus, I didn't want to get drunk again. Not after Jasper's letter."

"You'll be okay. It's a long time till the meeting."

"He said I was a drunk, dammit. That's what he said."

"He didn't, Urb. Not really. Now get in the car and I'll turn in the room key."

There was nothing to check out, so she simply slid the key across the desk and followed him through the twin entrance doors. Inside the car, he grew morose and silent. By the time they reached the summer place, he was slouched in sleep. He was still there, bent into multiple angles, the following morning. Not even the combined strength of Ruth, Clarice and Ramon had been able to move him or arouse him.

Recent meetings of the General Aid Fund board of directors had been reduced to rubber-stamping directives of its president. In spite of occasional dissents from Matthew Boylan, there really was little objectionable in regard to the financial progress of the telethon project more than two months in advance of its playing date. Several local corporations had already pledged fifty thousand dollars each, promising to match any additional sums donated by competitors. It was a strong start for Urban Giles Associates. He should have felt more heartened by it then he did.

"Nobody wants to go out there," Lederer called from New York. "It's going to be one bitch of a job getting the people you want."

Urban shuddered at that. His entire strength lay in the telethon itself—in his New York ability to produce a spectacle of star proportion at least approaching his past performances in the East. Without that, without a truly big show, it was possible his contract could be invalidated and the major percentage of his fee withheld. It was a grim shadow clouding his summer. Only Clarice knew its size and significance.

She had been more distant, less concerned than usual, distracted by their other involvements. Pleasure was a dangerous sensation. Not everyone was capable of handling it, of keeping it properly apportioned. It first amazed and then distressed Urban to see how childlike she became when the boy toyed with her. "You act like a goddamn high school girl," he complained. "For God's sake, Clarice, hold yourself together." She found statements like that ironic, coming from him. But she recognized the accuracy of some of them. It was just that she did not care. Not for now. Not in regard to Ramon.

There were no outward overtures between them, certainly not in public. He was an athletic boy on the beach, displaying the disinterest in things feminine, typical of his age. And she was a reasonably discreet woman with moments of doubt about all of it—its

wisdom, its morality, its success. Success. That somehow troubled her most. She did not like the thought
that he might not be physically attracted to her, submitting to her more in fondness and gratitude than lust.
Performance under adverse conditions was a simple
matter at his age. Potency was so easily tapped it took
little more than a ride in a car, preferably over a
bumpy road, to spring an ejaculation. She was aware of
that. It disturbed her that he might not want her at all,
just as she had begun to delude herself that he was in
love with her. That, she still was able to warn herself,
was dangerous.

Urban, by the same token, opposite side, was convinced his own masterful foreplay and mature finesse
truly did arouse Maria. Mildly so. He had even held
back percentages of himself for fear he was driving the
girl to borders of madness in her desire for him. There
were definite psychological advantages in such a dura-
ble ego.

"Lederer's starting to panic," he said to Clarice
when he no longer could carry the news alone. They lay
sprawled on the small triangle of private beach adjoining the house. It was shaded from the yacht club
property by a row of overhanging bushes. But they
were still visible through the tangle of roots if anyone
cared to spy on them.

"He always panics," she said. "He's like an old
woman in that job." Her eyes were unreadable behind
the dark hoops of her sunglasses. She was annoyed at
him for permitting himself to attain an erection, semi-
publicly, while watching Maria frolic in the sand. But
it had disappeared with his thoughts of Lederer. Sex

and survival were incompatible topics for simultaneous consideration.

"Nobody wants to come here," he continued. "You know what'll happen if they don't. We'll be wiped out."

"Give him a bigger cut. He's like a whore, Urb. Money's all he's after."

"You've got to remember he's not the president of W and W. He's just his assistant."

"So what? He imitates his voice perfectly. He's got access to all the files. He knows where the bodies are buried, who's being canceled, who's being renewed. He's got the stationery, he's even got the same secretary . . . it's all the same as it was before as far as we're concerned——"

"In New York, yes. In Toledo, I wonder."

"You're losing part of yourself here. You never ran scared like this before."

He turned on his side, feeling the rough sand grate into his skin. Maria came over to them and asked permission to go with Ramon to a soft-drink stand several hundred yards down the beach. He noticed absently how much she had matured physically in only the few months there. But he kept his observation to himself, rolling further until he was on his stomach. If there were any further extensions of himself they would be buried in the sand.

"Be careful," Clarice cautioned. "Some of those boys are not nice." As a parent, one could not be too careful these days. Drugs were appearing everywhere and it worried her. The two of them, sister and brother, scampered happily down the beach.

"Don't say anything about Lederer to Ruth this afternoon," she said when they were gone.

"She coming over again? Christ!"

"You should know. You invited her."

Ruth Fuller had seized upon the summer-long presence of the Giles family as a means of combatting her own loneliness. Elliot had become more than usually confined by his own family obligations with two daughters scheduled to be married within six weeks of one another.

Neither of them was accustomed to such frequent penetration into their private lives. No one in Manhattan or Elmhill enjoyed such random privileges with them. Ironically, it had been forced upon them by circumstances at just the time they most sought to avoid it. Ramon and Maria were still too young to faithfully practice the measured speech, the carefully filtered dialogue with outsiders, necessary in maintaining a secret life. Urban had made an extra effort to stress the naturalness of their way of life to keep them from becoming in any way upset or unduly curious about comparing it. "Keep family matters in the family," he told them. "That's the way nice people do it." His concern now was that they might interpret the frequency of Ruth's visits, and her occasional overnight stays, as admission to the family circle of confidence.

They transferred themselves to the yacht club's patio when Ruth arrived. It overlooked the club beach and marina, with the additional advantage of cocktail service to those in bathing suits. In a sense, a very real sense, it was a voyeur's paradise. All eyes were neutralized by sunglasses.

"Ramon's developing into a fine looking boy," Ruth said when he left the table, Coke in hand, and headed for the beach. Her head remained fixed toward the location of his sand arcobatics as she talked. Once again, Clarice experienced the strange sensation she refused to acknowledge as jealousy.

"He'll make a good football player one day," Urban said.

"No," Clarice objected. "I don't want that. He's built more like a swimmer."

"I think Clarice is right. Swimmers have those nice, smooth muscles—not the big, bulgy kind." Ruth whipped off her glasses to make a clear-eyed, unobstructed appraisal of the subject. "Yes, definitely. Ramon's the swimmer type."

It happened again to Clarice. The same adrenalin quickening her pulse, flushing the epidermis below her tan. She was embarrassed within herself at her own reaction.

Maria stretched herself on a beach towel, hardly in need of sun because of her natural complexion, yet prostrating herself before it nevertheless in a ritual known to peoples of all colorations.

Ruth now turned to her, glasses pushed upward into the thickness of her hair. She sipped slowly from her tall glass, watching her lie there, legs angled and apart, her suit indented along the middle of its crotch giving it a readily identifiable contour. "You know, it's impossible, but I swear Maria's grown up a year in just the few weeks I've known her," she said.

"You mean she's blossomed, don't you? More there than one might suspect?" Urban tried to play his hand with casualness to avert any suspicions. Guilt had a way of surfacing unless one kept constant check on all its edges.

Clarice hid in her drink, icing her lips with its cubes. Ruth was laughing, a small, shrill, piccolo laugh only she knew was an indicator of libido interest. She had gone with a man once who had confessed he invariably sneezed when he was thinking lewd thoughts. It was only to him she had confided her own tendency to laugh, almost giggle, in an upper register when her own mind was invaded by similar contemplations.

"How old is Maria now?" Ruth questioned.

"Almost fourteen."

"Almost a woman then."

"Almost," Urban agreed.

Maria turned over in the sun, revealing her derriere to be equally as well done as her frontal area.

"You're going to have trouble with her," Ruth said.

"Why, Ruth?" Clarice could no longer retain her muteness.

"Just look at her. She's actually voluptuous already."

"But she's just a baby, Ruth."

"Clare! Next you'll be saying the same about Ramon."

It was an incendiary accusation, harmless in intent but wounding in a sensitive area.

"You like him, don't you, Ruth?"

That was all she said, all manner of thoughts and frustrations compacted into a simple rhetorical question. A woman of less insight, of less experience, would not have discerned so many shades of meaning in a single flash of illumination. Nor would a lesser woman than Clarice have also realized immediately the full range of implications in her own few words. It was a tribute to their separate intelligences that both of them knew instantly the degree of exchange achieved by Clarice's remark. It had accomplished the difficult act of total communication.

If there was any next move, it was up to Ruth. Clarice could say no more to clarify the situation. Any attempt to juggle it into jest or expand it into a longer, less pointed observation would be an insult to Ruth's perceptiveness.

Urban suffered the tense silence, then waved for the pool boy who was also patio waiter, spinning his finger over the table to indicate another round, then finally looking off wistfully toward the horizon.

The children rejoined them before conversation resumed, postponing any showdown. Ruth had reacted in ladylike fashion, her claws covered despite the temptation to engage in what she now believed would be a most revealing catfight. "How do you like it here, Ramon?" she asked instead. She placed her hand on the smooth expanse of his inner thigh with deliberate intent.

"I like it," he said.

"I'll bet you haven't seen all the beautiful boats tied up at the marina, have you?"

"No."

"Would you like me to take you aboard some of them?"

His eyes skipped quickly from Urban to Clarice. There was no objection from either of them. "Yes," he said.

"And you, Maria? Would you like to come, too?"

She shook her head, her black hair swinging like pendulums on both sides of her face. "I don't like boats too much," she said.

Ruth got up and took Ramon's hand. "All right, then it's just you and me, Ramon." She looked directly at Urban and Clarice. "We'll be back in a little while. All right?"

After what had preceded the invitation, they were only too glad to please her. "Enjoy yourselves," Urban said as Clarice smiled weakly.

Ruth and the boy disappeared behind the boathouse, toward the spidery pontoon walks leading to the boats. Urban turned from them to his wife. He could see the question marks in her eyes. "Have another drink," he said. "You need it."

Maria studied both of them as they sat silently. Or so it seemed to Urban. "We'll take a walk, too," he promised. "Right after Daddy finishes his drink."

Many summers at the club with Elliot Ruskin had resulted in many friends for her there. She had no difficulty securing the permission of one captain to board the yacht of his employer, who was away in Europe. The boat, really large enough to be called a ship, was a magnificent Matthews cruiser. It had been constructed by hand only a few miles east of Toledo, custom-built to the owner's specifications. The captain excused himself to return to the patio cocktail lounge, confident in his trust of Ruth Fuller after having seen her in the company of Elliot Ruskin and his boss on so many occasions.

Ruth was an enthusiast. She reacted to Ramon's awe and wonder with proper proportions of her own enchantment at the yacht's gleaming brass fittings, the compasses and engine-room controls, its intricate radar devices, its flying bridge, its luxurious carpetings and mahogany furnishings.

He was still in his bathing trunks, providing her with unexpectedly revealing glimpses of himself as he strained for close-up views of certain accessories high above him or bent to touch the smooth swoop of the hull below him.

"One of these days you'll have a ship just like this," she said. "Would you like that?"

"Yes," he answered without hesitation.

She permitted him to roam the deck freely for a time, watching him intently. "Come here a minute, Ramon," she said after several minutes. He stepped over to her expectantly. "You're such a handsome young man, I just wanted to feel your muscles."

He grinned, feeling more comfortable with her than he ever had before.

"Make them hard for me once," she requested. "Like prizefighters and weight lifters do."

He angled his arms obediently, steeling the biceps until they were rigid hills on his upper arms. She ran her fingers caressingly over them several times. Abruptly, she clasped his shoulders and pushed her mouth fully into his lips.

"Have you ever made love to a woman, Ramon?" Her breath was heavy, her face still rising directly before his.

"Yes." Candor was automatic. He had not yet learned to lie.

"With Clarice?"

His embarrassment was obvious. She did not need

the reply verbalized. It made her feel triumphant, but she concealed her elation. "I want you to make love to me, too."

Her hands slid inside his trunks, under the mesh supporter, probing for his cock and balls. His prick rose in quick spasms at the invasion, making it more difficult to skin off the tight suit. It finally fell to the deck and he stepped from it with ballet grace.

In a matter of seconds, she freed herself, her breasts springing from their halter as though leaping hurdles. With the expertise of a woman accustomed to slithering in and out of girdles and garter belts, she writhed from the bottom half of her suit, kicking it aside as it fell, encircling his lean body like a tree she intended to climb. They merged without difficulty, settling into a frantic prologue before slowing to a more sustainable rhythm. Taking the lead in their dance, she inched them toward a shipside bunk, fucking continually in the process of the move. Once there, she dropped back and scissored his torso with her legs, squeezing him as though extracting the last drop of juice from a pliable container.

One prone, the other supine, they both climaxed readily, his come oysterish white and clammy against her hot skin, tiny pearls of it clinging like winter rain to the forest of her crotch. Her own resolution was the most delicious she could recall since her earliest experiences in sex—the result of her visual pleasure in him, his youth, his energy, and his surprisingly mature thrust and technique.

"Suck my tits for a while, please?" She fumbled one of them to him with her hands, its nipple plum-colored and ripe, a melon halved, its stem still intact. He slathered it with wet tongue, teasing it into further hardness with the tip of it, retracting the rest of her with the sharp pleasure of it.

"Do you like to fuck me, Ramon?"

He bobbed his head up and down without breaking contact. "Will you do it to me again, soon?" He nodded once more, watching himself enter and retreat from the bushy intersection of her legs.

"Fuck me," she whispered. It was pleasant to hear her own voice enunciating the taboo word which she never used without being naked. It was not ladylike, she contended. And, after all, she was nothing if not a lady.

"Have you ever done it to Maria?" Her body stiffened at the suggestion and she pushed forcefully into him. His eyes flashed under their long lashes.

"No," he said. "Never."

"Has Urban?"

He stopped momentarily, then drove into her with silent fury. Once more she had an answer without a spoken word. The wickedness of it all, herself now included, strummed her body, tensing it again, stirring it toward a new crescendo. "Get over my face," she ordered him hoarsely. "I want to suck your beautiful cock."

He was suspended over her almost immediately, lowering his genitals into her mouth, much of them spilling over her lips, an abundance of tender, rosy flesh to feast upon. She squirreled the balls in the pouches of her cheeks as though they were nuts, hard and unshelled yet smooth and coral pink, releasing them finally, reluctantly, to make room for the lacquered splendor of his taut cock, inserting the tip of her tongue into the tiny mouth of it before gorging herself on the full measure of it. She slid about it, painting invisible spiral stripes on a barber pole, then fell full-mouthed over all of it again, her head nodding yes-yes-yes-yes-yes-yes while her lips sealed the vacuum, breathing life and strength into the cock, a man with a life of his own attached to the body of a boy, a parasite siphoning virility and returning joy, a tense, throbbing muscle of flesh waiting to be conquered, wanting to be conquered, crammed to its tip with the hot lava of love.

Rich cream splashed against the roof of her mouth, coating its sides, trickling from its corners. He had difficulty maintaining balance, depleted by the suction of her. She broke the glycerin chain linking them, a kind of transparent umbilical cord, and fell to the side of him as he collapsed, both of them drawing in deep, lung-filling breaths. She patted him then, patting him later when he stretched fully on the deck, traveling the entire length of his body with her hands.

"Better get your suit on, dear," she said. "The captain could be coming back anytime now." It was unlikely, but so was the situation. He could not remain away indefinitely, despite a fondness for liquor, with two people wandering about the ship for which he was responsible.

She pulled on her suit in swift, adroit moves, hardly thinking about anything, still basking in the warm massage they had experienced. A moment after they reached the main deck, the captain appeared on the catwalk fingering from the central pier. "Stay aboard,

Miss Fuller," he called cheerfully. "I'd like to mix you a drink."

It was an appealing suggestion. It would give her a logical explanation for their long absence. "Thank you," she said. "I'd like that."

He was slim and athletic for his age, about the same as her own, vaulting onto the deck with practiced ease. "Ready to sign aboard, mate?" he asked Ramon, raking his fingers through the boy's midnight hair.

Ramon retreated back into shyness, merely nodding.

"He'll get over that," the captain said jokingly. "Just wait till he finds out about girls."

By the time they got back to the patio, the others were gone. The pool boy informed her they had complained of too much sun and were returning to the house. The sun had been down for some time but it was still light.

She had all her excuses set. All her explanations for their long absence. What she did not have in order were her own thoughts and emotions. It had been a revolutionary afternoon.

Chapter Ten

Lake weekends became fewer with the advent of August. It became less and less possible for all of them to escape Toledo together with the pressures of the approaching telethon. Elliot did arrange for charter flights several times in order that all four of them could enjoy at least an occasional day together at the summer house. But, finally, it became more strain than pleasure engineering the brief escapes. He volunteered as a compromise to his original plan to sail his cruiser down the Detroit River, into Lake Erie, and dock on the Maumee River. This way, he assured them, the Giles family could at least be together some evenings.

Ruth's interest in the children pleased Elliot. It relieved him at least partially of the previous need constantly to entertain her. One of his daughters was now married, one still remained to haunt him with the details and problems of her late August wedding. Life refused to allow itself to be paced, he decided. He had never been so inundated with such diverse responsibilities as he had been this summer. His only consolation was the progress of the telethon—thanks, he was quick to admit, to the professionalism of Urban Giles Associates. There was seemingly nothing they could not arrange—provided, of course, there was sufficient capital with which to expedite it.

Away from Elliot, masks off, Urb and Clare were walking one tightrope after another. They suspected Ruth Fuller's involvements with Ramon, yet both hesitated to question or chastise him. It might lead to further discoveries. Being busy had been a saving grace in that respect. There had been little opportunity for the kind of long, loose drinking sessions common to their earlier acquaintance—sessions fraught with the danger of self-revelation and incrimination. And she had been content to have her way with the boy, not certain what they knew, either. Still, the trump card seemed to be in her possession and they were forced to respect that probability.

Nightmaring their days, too, was Steven Lederer's increasingly vague and pessimistic attitude regarding delivery of celebrities for the show. It was a mounting agony for him, lessening all other interests almost to impotency. Clare also had become infected by the subliminal mood. The frivolity he had accused her of was gone. Reality had returned behind the advance force of jealousy. Perhaps it was a good thing the new family setup aboard Ruskin's boat prohibited continuation of their previous sleeping arrangements.

"What about Dennis Devlin?" Clarice wondered aloud. They were brooding alone in the stillness of their cabin, long after the children were asleep.

"He stinks, Clare. You know that."

"He's a good crier. Pay him his price and he'll sob out pledges."

"People are sick of him. He's on every show going—every telethon, every benefit. . . ."

"This is Toledo, Urb."

"Stop reminding me."

"How about Lisa Scott?"

"She's a bitch. Remember how she held us up for more money while the show was on—while all those crippled kids were sitting around listening?"

"You keep telling me we're not running a picnic. We can't do it with angels and saints."

"I'd rather shoot for some less obvious types. Like Betty Chaplin, for instance."

"Talk about bitches!"

Urban rolled on his side and addressed the thick blackness. "They're all whores, but what do we care? What goes up on those tote boards is what counts. Bleed the bastards. Make them cry. Make them feel guilty. That's what our business is all about, Clare."

She sighed deeply. "You're right. Let's try to get Scott and Chaplin."

"At least they're pros."

"So's Devlin."

"All right. What the hell. I'll call him myself. To-morrow." He rolled back the other way, the front of his body now angling into the rear of her. The soft tubing of his crotch sandwiched into the valley of her buttocks. He made a few tentative bump-and-grind motions, more playfully than seriously.

"Uh-uh," she said.

"How long's it been?"

"Whatever, it's got to be a little longer."

He teased her with a simulation of intercourse, pumping steadily into the crevice of her.

"I said stop it."

"You're misquoting yourself. You said it had to be a little longer. It's getting longer."

"You know I meant time." It was strange, but under this circumstance, even after all their years together, she was not certain if he was serious or not. The distraction of playing an old game was rather welcome after business, even though she was honestly disinterested in his teasing. At least in the possible truth behind it.

He had begun reaching under her, inserting the tips of four fingers into the wet crack between her thighs, pushing his lengthening penis into the opening he had made. Having gone this far, both of them began to get interested.

"You've been in tighter places lately," she said, warming more to the game now that he was fingering her clitoris above the angle of his cock.

"You've had harder guests, too," he said.

In a matter of minutes he was solid. They settled into a back-and-forth, to-and-fro syncopation in unexpected harmony with one another. There in the darkness, mating like night animals, it was a simple matter to entertain any fantasies necessary to climax.

Resolved, they turned back-to-back like bookends, momentarily rescued from their cares, and slipped steeply into sleep.

Urban was pulled up short in the yo-yo looping of his life with the impossible news that Steven Lederer had been fired. He had already advanced him seven thousand dollars of their limited budged—unrecorded, undeductible, unaccountable, now uncollectable dollars. His ego was hit as hard as his purse.

The report left him out on a plank, blindfolded, fumbling for direction. He decided to call New York and personally plead with Lederer's boss. After all, it was a legitimate proposal. Only Lederer's role in it was illegitimate.

"I'll see if Mr. Whitcomb is in," the secretary said coolly. She had received all his calls before with cheerful receptiveness. Her voice disappeared now into the vapors of long distance, replaced by relays of electronic sounds. When it returned, it was even colder. "Mr. Whitcomb is sorry but he is busy and unable to comment at this time on any matters initiated in his name by Mr. Lederer," she said.

He buried the phone in its cradle. The money was really secondary. It had been siphoned from funds never allocated directly to the Giles operation, although he could have used them handily himself. More importantly, he had lost his primary contact in the founding and structuring of his telethons.

Clarice's tan seemed to bleach at the news. "I never trusted Steve," she said. Hindsight has a way of being profound, he noted in his own distress.

"Get on the phone," Urban ordered. "Dial everybody we know. Dennis, Betty—all those people. We've got to get some talent booked or you can book me into Calvary." There was no humor in his word play.

The afternoon in the arcade flashed before him and retreated. He was at the nadir of his existence now, not then. He stood in the middle of the office like a tree, tallest before its axing, his hands fluttering leaflike from the ends of his arms, branching helplessly outward, anticipating a certain fall.

"Urban." Her voice seemed to be knelling. He swung about, his face a gallows mask.

"What else?"

"It's a hell of a time, but it can't wait."

His eyes closed and his face tightened further. "All right," he said softly. "Don't let it wait then."

"Maria is pregnant," she said.

The car had been coughing; now it stuttered briefly and stopped. He got out as if he were bailing out, his body hunched, bent, folded, pitching forward into a small rise of embankment next to the highway. The car's headlights painted long corridors into the blackness, ending in dim rings against an empty backdrop. He crawled back into the car and turned the ignition key, silencing the engine, then jammed the protruding plunger against the dashboard, extinguishing the lights.

Where the hell am I? he asked himself. The question prodded him with left and right jabs to his brain, making his ears ring. He fingered the tall grass rising in the ditch as though it might provide a clue, knowing even as he did it that it was the grass of the world, everywhere-grass of no special distinction.

He lowered himself into it slowly, still stunned by the suddenness with which he had spun off the road, still wound in the emotional bandages of the night before. The blades of grass reached for his face, razor-edged in one direction, caressing in the other. Where had it begun again? He remembered the drinks at the Hotel Renslow, he remembered saying good night to Ruth Fuller and wondering at the strangeness of her mood, he remembered stopping off at the boat and excusing himself to Clare on the premise of a private meeting with a board member. God, he could remember everything if he kept trying. After that came the crossing, greeting the United States customs guard on the bridge from Detroit, U.S.A., into Windsor, Canada. He had stopped somewhere then, at some hotel bar, harshly lit and almost empty. It was there the murkiness had set in.

So he was very likely still in Canada. Probably Ontario. It was so simple to leave America, so much more difficult to reenter. He got up again, unsteadily, and looked around. On a night as bleak as this, the whole world must look the same, he decided.

His knowledge of mechanical devices was decidedly limited. But he fumbled about until he was able to raise the hood and peer into the car's engine. It was blurred by darkness, looking like a forged intestinal track. The lack of light hardly mattered. It was as clear to him under these conditions as it would have been under a noonday sun. He slammed the hood cover down and returned to the driver's seat, flicking the ignition switch on. This time he recognized his plight. The fuel indicator was all the way to the left, asleep on an empty tank.

An hour passed before another car approached and stopped. "You all right, sir?" the driver asked. He was a Canadian accustomed to the late night vicissitudes of his native land. Because of it, he carried a five-gallon can of gasoline in his trunk. Generously, he offered half of it to Urban. They poured it into the tank and the man gave him directions to an all-night filling station some twenty miles away. He refused any compensation for the gasoline, not even the price he had paid.

"Glad to help out," he said pleasantly. The gesture penetrated even the fog of Urban's partial reality. He could not help thinking how far removed the man was from the corruption which he accepted as a fact of life.

The Canadian escapade lasted three more days, creating the first really serious damage to his reputation in the eyes of Elliot Ruskin. Perhaps the warning from that reporter had been right.

Urban attempted to dismiss his absence under the guise of a telethon talent search. But the trembling of his hands, the blotched dissipation of his face contradicted his own testimony.

"Don't let me down, Urban," Ruskin said solemnly. "We've gone too far now to turn back."

Trouble was all over him now. Like poison ivy, the more he rubbed, the more it spread.

One of them would have to go back to New York with the girl. There was really not much of a problem attached to being pregnant anymore. Not if it was detected early enough. They estimated Maria to be somewhere around her eleventh week, which put her within simple abortion time limits.

"I'll take her," Clarice insisted. "She should have a woman along."

"It might be better if I went," Urban said. "I could see Lederer that way."

"We're talking about two different things. Somebody has to stay with her."

He looked dismal, but it was not due to the girl. "We'll both go," he decided. "Ray can stay with Ruth."

Clarice had lost some of her fortitude, some of her ability to challenge him, in the recent drain of their finances and the threat of further problems. It had never occurred to her so completely before, but she was aware all at once how much a part money played in the structure of life beyond the mere economics of it. Her resistance, the march of her libido, had been halted simultaneously and detoured in new directions. With them had gone the petty jealousies as well. Ruth could serve a purpose now. Why not utilize her?

"You can't leave this situation up in the air for long," she warned him.

"Give me three days."

"I haven't told Maria any details yet," she said.

His face turned grainy and his eyes appeared mulched. "For crissake, Clare, do you want me to do it? Get it over with."

"I feel awful about it."

He was still frayed and tense from his Canadian interlude. His overcast eyes turned stormy. "Whatever you do, Clare, don't turn pious on me. You said the pills worked."

"They always did on me."

His laugh was taunting. "You can't test a dam in a desert," he said.

Her eyes flashed, intersecting his. "Never mind the dam, dammit. This is your fault. I'm sick of it, leading your life. It's not my life, god dammit, it's not my life at all!"

He had never heard her voice erupt so suddenly loud. Nor had he ever seen her vibrate so violently, her body shaking, water spilling from her eyes.

"I'm sorry, Clare," he said. "We're both all wound up, I guess."

She retreated from his effort to grasp her, pitching herself forward onto the couch. He stood by helplessly, appealing to the ceiling for aid, then left the room.

They departed for New York the following day. The processional to the plane's boarding stairs was smileless and silent, almost funereal. It took all the miniature martinis he could muster from nondrinking passengers to raise him to the level of ordinary existence. His mind was all Lederer, all doom. The matter of Maria, sitting with Clarice in the row before him, was the least of his concerns.

Ruth Fuller was delighted to be appointed Ramon's chaperone. She had seen him infrequently since their afternoon aboard the yacht. Elliot had kept her traveling for weeks, almost as though he knew of the encounter. Which, of course, he did not. She had relived it often since in torrid sessions with herself, her facial massager plunged deep within her or simply flicking the tender erection of clitoris. It succeeded in driving her into collisions of climaxes resembling those of her afternoon with Ramon, the sweet violence of which she had not experienced since adolescence.

"Remember our day on the boat?" she asked at the first opportunity.

"Uh-uh," he said without looking up from the car racing magazine he was intently studying.

She stroked his back as he read, sprawled on the deck, his white twill pants molding the rise of his buttocks. Her hand slipped under the loose sheath of his polo shirt and traveled the valley between his shoulder blades. He rippled his spine at her touch, twisting his body as though trying to shrug her away. But she persisted.

Ruth was kind to him in the way all women past their primes are kind to attractive young men. She forgave his indifference to her at the moment as a temporary condition. She wanted only to have him connect himself to her, however briefly, and renew her own confidence in her ability to attract the attractive. The compromises and conditions under which it was accomplished mattered little.

"What do you like best—boats or cars?" Her face was next to his now, pretending equal absorption in the illustrations before them.

"Both."

"Isn't that something—you're on a boat and you're reading about cars."

He turned and ignited a smile. "When I'm in cars, I read about boats."

She pawed him kittenishly and he retaliated with a light wrestling hold. Breaking it, she rolled against him and clutched his crotch. They had gone beyond subtleties together before. There was no sense wasting time with them now.

The surprise grab scissored his body and he laughed at the shock pleasure of it. "No fair," he said.

"What's no fair?"

"Grabbing my meat." It was an expression he had picked up around school. He had never used it with an adult before.

"I thought they were jewels," she responded.

He was on his back, shielding himself between the legs with cupped hands. She crawled over to him on all

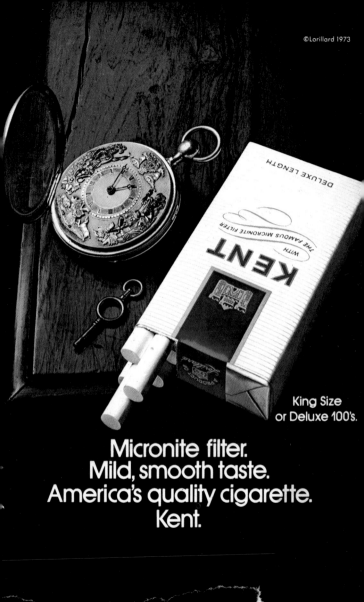

©Lorillard 1973

King Size
or Deluxe 100's.

Micronite filter.
Mild, smooth taste.
America's quality cigarette.
Kent.

Try the crisp, clean taste of Kent Menthol.

The only Menthol with the famous Micronite filter.

fours, her breasts hanging low, sloshing against one another as she moved. It was far from an executive posture, but she felt wonderfully alive and expectant in it. "Let's take our clothes off. It's more fun playing that way."

"Make me," he challenged her. The Gileses had instilled in him a special sense of freedom.

She leaped over him, releasing the locks on the hinges of her arms and legs when she was directly above him, landing like a covey of water-filled balloons over most of his body, thrashing and clawing and pulling at his clothes, shredding the shirt from his back, forcing the zipper of his pants to part, a metal river turned aside by an onrushing force, slicing her hands between the layers of flesh and fabric, fondling the smooth skin of his lower body, saving the best of him until at last she had all of him again.

His chest heaved from a sudden release of energy, a tawny bellows dotted with two burgundy nipples, corrugated by even rows of ribs, the navel a small pond centered with a pink island, a landmark on the road to his treasures.

She was breathing hard, salivating, a potpourri of juices bubbling within and without, her appetite whetted by the sight of the feast and her invitation to begin. Restraining herself to heighten the pleasure, she began slowly to consume him, writing her name with her tongue on his abdomen in the vanishing ink of saliva, circling his navel and flicking the miniature rise within it, then traveling due south to the edge of his pubic hair, sweeping north again, south again, north again, digging an imaginary gulley, drawing an invisible path to the magic forest. Finally, stealthily, she entered it, breathing in the electric curls as though they were life-giving, brushing her lips against them to light her way, lingering amidst them, fighting the temptation from the hard root of him indenting her cheek. Her tongue emerged again, swooping about the base of it, descending rather than climbing, her mouth opening to receive the twin eggs of his manhood, cradling them in the moist cave beyond her lips, sucking them as though she could draw their contents into her.

He was very quiet, stilled by the soft pulsations bubbling in his body, wondering at the chemistry stirring within him, pooling his resources for another launch of himself. She had begun licking the length of his cock, hands rounding the base of it, fingering the balls, seeming to swallow the head of it repeatedly, only to have it reappear—an indestructible, undiminishable lollipop. He tensed abruptly, lifting himself partially to meet the recoil of his own body, his move inspiring her to such feverish action her head blurred before him. He came then, in quick, stuttering shots, oiling the roof of her mouth, filling the opening to her throat, forcing her to rip him from her lips, a final shot streaking like a tracer bullet into the air, arcing to the deck several feet away.

She climbed upward onto him now, her lips still sweet with the liqueur of him, determined to suck the last molecule of solidity from him with her body, hopeful of keeping it hard with renewed action. "Fuck me," she said, pleased by his continuing firmness, wanting now to savor the joy of climax within herself.

He pressed into her fiercely, arching his back, vibrating himself at a rapid rate, meeting her own frenzied pumping in sharp impacts, collapsing finally under the weight of her, rolling sideways at the direction of her guiding hands, continuing there, side by side, until she began to groan loudly, her body shuddering and finally stopping, stopping, until it was totally still.

"Oh," she said a long time later. "That was good, good, good." With that, she kissed him on his neck, his shoulders, his hair. "Thank you, Ramon, love," she said.

All the next day was spent planning for the next night. At least, as far as Ruth Fuller was concerned. His education had to proceed. He had mastered the elementary level. Now she would graduate him into the oral division. The thought of it was so enormously pleasurable to her she could not function in the office at all that day.

"How is your baby-sitting working out?" Elliot asked offhandedly.

"Why?" she challenged, a trifle too defensively.

He was surprised by the snap of her response. His eyes arched, the brows two bridges suspended over his face. "Why indeed? Something wrong?"

"Oh, no. No. Not at all."

"Are you sure, Ruth? I can easily get someone to take over the assignment if it's too much for you." He touched her shoulders affectionately. "I know it's been a rough summer. We'll get away somewhere after the telethon, I promise you."

She touched his hand in return, grateful he thought she was under some special stress because of him. "Thank you, Elliot. You're always so sweet."

At the earliest moment possible, she ducked out of the office and headed for the pier. Strangely, for the first time she could recall, it felt as though she was bubbling and frothing between her legs. It was a feeling at once wet and hot and good.

Ramon had been alone much of the day under the casual supervision of the dock superintendent. There were several girls his own age scattered about other boats moored there and she felt vaguely envious of them as she approached. Was she jealous? She laughed at the thought.

"What have you been doing all day?" she greeted him.

"Reading mostly."

"Cars?"

A smile split his bronze face.

"Did you think about last night?"

"Some."

"So did I. I thought a whole lot about it." She enjoyed the interrogation of him and wanted it to continue. It had an odd, erotic effect upon her. "Did you do anything with yourself like that?"

He looked away. "A little."

"Don't be ashamed. There's nothing wrong with it. Everybody does it."

"Supposed to make you go crazy," he grinned.

She laughed throatily. "No wonder everybody's nuts," she said.

They were getting along famously and it pleased her. "Tonight we're going to do something different. A new game."

"Okay."

Being an instructress was a most satisfying role. She was anxious now to get on with the class demonstration. "Let's go inside," she said. "You must be hungry."

"A little."

She had never dealt much in *double entendre* before, not in the staid insurance business. It was fun to let herself go. "I've got something nice for you to eat," she said.

He followed her into the main cabin and watched as she drew the blinds on all sides and slipped the latch on the door. Then she positioned herself on a chair, draping her legs over the two armrests, exposing the full irrigation of her thighs, her sheath pulled up and gathered at her waist, providing a circular silk frame for the damp nest between her legs. "Here it is," she said, interrupted by the sight of the bulge against the entrance to his pants. She *had* aroused him. It was another source of pleasure in a day filled with thoughts of it.

"Take off your clothes, love," she instructed. "I want to kiss you and I want you to kiss me."

He slipped easily from his clothes, sucking in his abdomen to overcome the angle of his erection, his pants then falling soundlessly to the deck. There had been no reaction from him to the last part of her statement and she wondered if he understood her. But he was there at her lips and she drew him into her mouth, forgetting the moment before in the fullness of the moment now.

It was a marvel to her, a reincarnation of youth for her, almost guiltless to her because of his physical maturity and now his willingness. She had been able to extract three encores from him in the past, the last of them more potent than the first from men her own age. His virility lathered her lust and she devoured all that was loose and removable about him, her tongue curling up his penis, reptilian, licking the glistening lubricant, feasting on the candied crown, diluting all of it in the sea of her mouth; restoring, polishing, giving and taking without damage to either of them, adding rather than subtracting, pleasure in place of pain. It was beautiful beyond words.

She reached up, the length of her arms, and pulled him downward, his face passing hers en route, then her breasts, her navel, until she brought it to a firm halt at the triangle of her legs, planting it positively into the moist bushiness. "Suck it, darling," she said.

He had never been face to face with it before, raw and red, wrinkled and layered, its entrance a maze of slippery skin panels, a pungent fragrance escaping from its hidden corridors. He stuck his face into it tentatively, as though searching for directions. She extricated him by his ears, peering down upon him like a mountain-breasted Buddha. "With your tongue, dear," she explained. She reached about, under herself, and opened the lips wide, creating a dark hole beyond them. "See this little thing?" she asked, pinching the small finger of skin comprising her clitoris. "It loves being tickled by your tongue."

This time he beveled his face into her again, tongue poised, and sought out the pink stalactite hanging from her cave, darting his tongue against it, catching the rhythm spontaneously, feeling her pitch forward from his contact, rolling with the undulations of her body, rising and falling, locked in the pillowed flesh of her thighs, plunging deeper into the mystery of her until, suddenly, dramatically, a feeling of *déjà vu* swept over him and he was home within her, the mystery solved.

She climaxed quickly, caught up in the entirety of her erotic panarorama, her body shuddering long moments after the orgasm, her eyes sealed to preserve the ecstasy. She got up slowly later, restoring herself to a semblance of dignity now that the aching lust was sedated.

"Tomorrow," she said, "they'll all be back from New York."

Even with the relaxed legislation, Clarice despised the primitive ritual of abortion procedure. There were still forms to fill out, outer-office squattings to be endured, stares to be returned or ignored, implications to be accepted or denied. Both doctors and nurses, despite their white-coated nonchalance, were still curious, inquisitive human beings. An abortion clinic was, after all, a kind of first-aid center off to the right or left of sexuality. Women and girls did not come there suffering from external wounds, bruises or contusions. They were there because they had been penetrated. In the vitals.

"How old are you, dear?" the receptionist inquired.

"Thirteen. Almost fourteen," Charice said.

The woman behind the desk escalated her gaze, brimmed and lowered it. "I would prefer it if the patient gave the answers," she said stiffly.

"Thirteen, going on fourteen," Maria said.

"Is this your mother?"

Eyes elevated again, skin tones registering. "Is this your natural or adoptive mother?"

"I don't know."

"Adopted," Clarice said.

The woman did not look up from the form. "And your father is Urban Giles?"

"Yes."

"Natural father?"

"Adopted," Clarice repeated.

The woman's eyes spiraled. "Wait here," she said and disappeared into the adjoining hall.

Whatever thoughts or analyses might have occurred to her, whatever doubts now rose in Clarice, everything from that moment on went according to the prescribed plan. The child within the child was aborted easily. Forty-eight hours of recovery, five hundred dollars of cash, and Maria Giles was eviscerated, ready for her next encounter.

Only Clarice suffered any aftereffects.

Lederer was cold and elusive, a direct contrast to the virtually tactile humidity of metropolitan August. He had not wanted to meet with Giles at all, but he was in fear of the unknown since being dispossessed from his position with Whitcomb and Wiley. They met in a nondescript bar and grill on the west side of town to avoid any possibility of being seen together. The booths there were almost monastic in their hard barrenness, but they were private, surrounded by working men devouring beer-and-sandwich lunches—a good, safe place to indulge in specifics.

"I've spoken to Lou Whitcomb and everything's going to work out all right for you, Giles."

"I tried to call him the other day. He wouldn't even talk to me."

"He's upset. Just let me handle it."

"But you're out of it, Steve. What can you do now?"

"Whitcomb's not that big a prick. He's not going to hang you to get me. Besides, he's not even that mad at me. I might even get back with him."

"I wish I could believe you. I need that list. I need contracts from the people you promised."

"You'll get them, dammit. Whitcomb can't afford a big stink. He's okayed the deals with your people."

"I wish I could hear it from him."

"I'll remember that. Kicking a guy who's knocked himself out for you. You're making a big mistake, Giles. I'm in no way finished. Just don't get me hot or I will pull out the talent——"

Urban's eyes receded. "I've got to trust you, Steve. I do trust you. But I'm up against the wall now."

"Relax."

Perspiration beaded both their faces. A drab, monolithic air-conditioner alternately hummed and fluttered beside them, its huge size out of all proportion to the amount of coolness it was dispensing.

"I don't live in your world, Steve. I can't live on hors d'oeuvres and handshakes."

Lederer looked annoyed. "What's that supposed to mean?"

"I'm desperate, Steve. You've got to get me those contracts before I leave town."

"Impossible," he said coldly.

Urban ordered another double and downed it immediately. "I don't believe you can do it, but I have no other choice but to string with you now."

"Better cut down on the booze, Urban G. It's starting to get to you again." He lifted the small glass before him, surveying its brown surface as though it was a monocle he planned to insert in his eye. Then he brought it to his lips, savored it momentarily, and let the contents disappear between them. He sat silently waiting for the searing charge of it to detonate within him, his water glass clutched and ready to extinguish the flames. When it was over, the bombing and the quenching, he closed his eyes for a moment and lost himself elsewhere, shutting out Urban Giles, the trafficking in which they were engaged and the memory of his dismissal. Reopening them, he saw the fright lurking all about the man, a fleeting double exposure which captured him more completely than any focused look had done before. Instead of softening his attitude, it hardened it further.

"I need more cash," he said coldly.

Urban's eyes emptied, refilling with hatred and contempt. "You've already got more than you deserve," he said as evenly as he could. "You've got the guts to come here with a notice from Whitcomb, no artists delivered, and ask for more? What size balls have you got, Steve? They must be basketballs——"

"You want the people, I want the cash."

"I don't have any people!" Giles screamed.

Several of the workmen turned and looked curiously at them. "Like I told you about the booze. . . ."

Circles of perspiration darkened under Urban's arms at the repeated accusation. He had spent a lifetime swallowing the insults of men like Lederer and here he was forced to do it again. With an unemployed assistant to a president. The thought of it struck him as the ultimate humiliation.

"Where do we stand now?" he asked.

"I'll be back in the office for a few weeks, winding things up. Whitcomb knows about the show. I'll spend my full time on it until I leave. Like I said, *if* I leave." The implication stood out sharply.

"What do I do?"

"You'll hear from me when I get a check."

He was resigned through desperation. "How much?"

"Ten."

"Jesus, Steve, be realistic! I couldn't possibly get you more than five at this point."

"All right. I'm not hard to get along with. Five grand here tomorrow. At my house."

Urban rose wearily and shuffled with him toward the door, a terrible fear haunting his appended agreement with Lederer, still silken and unshaken by all that had happened to both of them. Outside in the searing heat he waited until Lederer had found an air-conditioned cab.

"Don't let me down, Steve," he said before the cab door closed. "I'm a father now."

Lederer smiled thinly from within, his fingers forming the old Winston Churchill victory sign. Then the yellow shell rounded a corner and he was gone.

Urban hesitated a moment, swung about and returned to the same saloon they had just left. It was the only way to prepare himself for the return to Toledo.

Chapter Eleven

No time remained to project or fantasize. The telethon was less than three weeks away; the papers were filled with promotional stories and pictures of Broadway and Hollywood stars scheduled to participate. Paradoxically, the flood of advance publicity, which he had largely arranged for himself, now worried him by its very abundance. His reputation was on the line—and that line was stretched as tautly as it could be without snapping.

Maria was all right, but not to be tampered with for a while. That was just as well with him. He was asexual in moments of stress anyhow.

Along with the publicity, the lineup of local high school bands, veterans' groups and amateur entertainers kept growing. It only increased his anxiety over Lederer's new evasiveness. "If nothing else," he said grimly, "we'll have one hell of a football half-time show." Not the faintest quiver of a smile accompanied the remark either.

Clarice had almost jumped from the plane, figuratively, when he told her of his meeting and new arrangement with Lederer. If Maria had not been there, requiring tranquility and attention, she might possibly have done just that.

"You're out of your mind, Urb. You must be crazy to trust that thief." She had been silent the whole trip, except for occasional comforting comments to Maria. On the way home in the car, she repeated her earlier evaluation of him. "You need a psychiatrist," she said. "I mean it sincerely."

She moved fully back into her old role as chief aide-de-camp after that. If this was to be their last stand, as she now envisioned, then they would have to go down fighting together.

Six girls were recruited from among dozens of applicants to handle the temporary secretarial and receptionist-clerking duties surrounding the final push at the field office of UGA. Thankfully, they had been able to secure the services of the "bleeding hearts team" of Dennis Devlin, Lisa Scott and Betty Chaplin despite their earlier reluctance to even contact them. They were now the only concrete names they could bandy about and their arrival in the city would at least provide a week of distraction for the press and other media. Naturally, they all required fees and per diem expenses. Elliot Ruskin, who was increasingly anxious and dubious as the date neared, hastily arranged an emergency expenditure from the finance committee. Three faces of some renown were better than no faces. At least for the time being.

"There'll be more, lots more," Urban continued to assure him. What else could he say? The entire show was entrusted to his experience and he had no choice but to move publicly with the assurance of a renowned producer on the verge of another hit. It was in the private moments, away from everyone but Clarice, that his panic almost asphyxiated him. Even there, he strove not to alarm her further.

"It's going to work out all right," he said repeatedly. "Everything's going to be all right." But he had no contracts from Lederer and he could not reach him by telephone. He had not returned to Whitcomb and Wiley as he had told Urban. And Whitcomb continued to refuse to talk to Giles or any representatives of UGA. "You will hear from our attorney," the secretary had relayed finally. There was no purpose in calling there after that.

"I only worry about the children," Clarice said equally as often as he assured her of things working out. It was her prompting which resulted in the family moving from the boat into a downtown hotel. The boat had been a lovely change of pace for all of them, she explained to Elliot, but in the final days before the telethon they wanted the children near at hand while they maintained round-the-clock work schedules. It was plausible; not even Ruth questioned it.

Urban was constantly in and out of strange telephone booths, armed with rolls of quarters, placing mysterious long-distance calls all over the country. Unable to find Lederer, he spent his last hours attempting personal liaison with the stars on the promised list. It was futile and he knew it. But like a man dying, his emotions hemorrhaging, he had to keep flailing at his unseen attackers until all life and hope were gone.

Ruth Fuller, oblivious to the internal strife, insisted on acting as liaison between the General Aid Fund board of directors and Urban Giles Associates as the hour of the great local fund-raising experiment approached. The atmosphere, tense enough without her, became a nightmare of additional frustrations for Urban with her entanglement.

He began drinking steadily two days before the show, seemingly unable to submerge his anxieties no matter how much he drank. But her companionship ultimately did succeed in getting him drunk and compounding the entire picture for him. They had gone to the family suite at the Lakeland Hotel after hours together. It was then that Ruth had done something she never would have considered in a sober state. She went into Ramon's room, brushed aside the thin sheet covering his sleeping figure, and kissed him—not on the lips but on the cock.

Urban had raged after her then, gathering the skin of her arms like loose yard goods in his hands, whiplashing her head with a sudden jolt backward. "Get your hands off him, you goddamn whore!" he screamed.

He pulled her into the yellow light of the hall and hurled her to the floor. Staggering to her feet, she realigned herself enough to strike him flush in the eye with a clenched fist, then fell upon him, pummeling him with both hands, screaming hysterically, "Bastard! Bastard! Bastard!," as the hard knots of her fingers rained upon him.

Clarice and Maria were awake by now, joining Ramon in the struggle to separate the two of them. "Ruth! Urban! My God, what's this all about? Stop it! Stop it!" Between all of them pulling at the disarray of their bodies, they finally managed to separate them. Their faces were rivered with gritty sweat and blood, their eyes a crazed and riveted collection of blue and red and brown.

"This is only the beginning," Ruth said brokenly as she lurched to the elevator. "You haven't heard the end of this, you bastard."

Clarice huddled the children off into the suite, her arms trembling terribly. They had been introduced to too much of adulthood already and it sickened her to realize the probable impact of this newest exposure.

"There's no sense talking to you now," she said to him when the furor had subsided and the children returned to bed. Her body felt empty at the sight of him, shaken and distraught, a thin trickle of blood seeping from the corner of his mouth.

"Don't worry about a thing," he mumbled.

After a struggle, she managed to undress him and push him into the shower, leaving him there with the water running. If she had known how to cry, she would have done so. But somewhere between youth and middle age, between the dreams of adolescence and the realities of menopause, she had forgotten how it was done.

What had begun as mainland, then narrowed into peninsula, was now an island. There was no turning back for any of them despite their differences. They were on a floe together, their only hope of rescue lying in the maintenance of some semblance of balance and unity.

Urban was a physical mess the morning after. As might be expected, he remembered little of the whole fracas. He blamed his appearance on muggers, but dismissed the suggestion that he report it to police. If it did not fool many, it at least sufficed as a quick retort to the inevitable questions about his appearance. "What happened?" was the question around every corner he turned.

No one was certain just how much Ruth Fuller recalled of the night. She simply withdrew from circulation, saving herself immediate explanations, implying by phone that she was victimized by that reliable feminine monthly invasion. No one ever seemed to chart the ebb and flow of these periods in women. Therefore, they retained a perpetual, unquestioned validity no matter how frequently the cycle seemed to recur.

Some of the careful control of Elliot Ruskin wavered in the midst of the turmoil. He was, however, too committed to the project to even dream of withdrawal. He could not even indicate apprehension except to Urban.

"I'm not going to get into that business with you and Ruth the other night," he confronted him. "But I am asking for your pledge as a person of responsibility that everything will go as contracted for this weekend."

A crippled smile struggled over Urban's face. "You have nothing to lose, Elliot," he said.

"That's a rather ominous simplification, Urban. I live and function in this city. If this telethon fails, I am the scapegoat with the board and with the public—not you. Your life continues elsewhere as before——"

"We all have the same credentials in the cemetery, Elliot."

"What's that supposed to mean?"

"Whatever you want it to."

Ruskin sighed deeply. "I'll tell you this. If I could

get out of this thing and save face, I'd do it right now."

"I would then, if I were you."

They were in a circular conversation, going nowhere; both too tired to devise a way out. Finally, Elliot formed a question. "Who have we got as of this moment? Positives."

"You have the list. It's the same one I have."

Ruskin laughed without humor. "Come now, Urb. Do we have a single, absolute, guaranteed major name?"

"I can't understand you. Three nationally known people are here right now. They've been here all week, touting the show on every program in town."

"What you're saying then is that's it. Those three people are it."

"I've explained to you a number of times as I have to all the board members—this is a crazy business. For this type of appearance, there are no standard contracts with performers . . . at least not the big ones. It's essential to them that the public believes they're on the telethon voluntarily—that they're making a charitable contribution to the betterment of mankind. We want it that way, too, don't we? Otherwise nobody'd kick in. They're not about to donate money to subsidize a big paid concert, can't you see? The deals, like the payoffs, have to be subtle and hidden. That's my department, Elliot, so please relax. . . ."

Ruskin pressed the wrinkles in his forehead with the flat of his hand. "I haven't seen a thing out of this myself as things stand. You realize that, don't you?"

They were back on Urban's favorite plateau. "Don't worry. There'll be enough for everybody."

"I must say you're as convincing as ever. Perhaps it's just that I believe you just a little less than originally."

"Clare has lined up some beautiful victims for the money pitches, Elliot. Take my word for it, that's where it's all at in the telethon business."

"I'd rather not know about that."

"See? It's my headache eventually, isn't it? So relax and let me handle all of it."

Ruskin could not convey the extent of his own inner torment. Their alliance had deteriorated, but so had he in the course of it. He fingered the letter in his inside pocket and recalled its key words. "Urban Giles is a man without conscience, schizophrenic, paranoid and alcoholic. I urge you and your fellow board members to reconsider any promotional enterprise involving either him directly or his firm. . . ." It was signed Floyd Jasper.

What bothered him most now was how it reflected upon himself. The shadows across his own presence were darkening by the minute.

Events, like railroad cars, had followed in orderly procession until the inevitable collision. Now bodies were being strewn everywhere, hasty decisions were being made, tempers flared and died, spirits sagged and collapsed. Urban operated on nerve ends, raw and exposed, his desperation muted by the need to appear collected and calm.

His company of experts had moved into the Paragon Theater by this time, supplemented by a variety of domestic and imported stage men. Most troublesome among them were the stage craft unions, demanding expanded contracts under threat of boycott and programming demolition. He met privately for two hours with the head of the city's musicians, emerging finally with a contract to play the show. The bluff was essential right up to countdown. He played touch and go with each of the other unions, fourteen in all, affixing his bold scrawl to each contract in turn.

In the midst of it, his eyes rung with sleeplessness, his face a rack on which all of the show's troubles were hung. Clarice slipped him a fresh clipping from the latest *Variety*. It was buried in the radio-television section but she had circled it with the outline of a skull and crossbones beneath it.

The caption was immediately frightening: AD EXEC'S T-THON CAPERS CAPON CAREER. Beneath those words, cryptic to a layman but all too graphic to him, were the telling details.

Steven Lederer, longtime top aide to Whitcomb & Wiley prexy Lou Whitcomb, ankled firm suddenly Tues. (11). Diverse reasons topped by reported arm-twisting of key W&W clients to guest on varied Urban Giles-produced telethons locally and elsewhere, currently Toledo, O. Celeb protests finally hurdled the Lederer screen, long effective in defusing and dousing tempers of front-rank video notables, sez a Whitcomb spokesman. No action planned beyond axing.

He made a jagged rip in the page, severing the piece with the story and stuffing it into his jacket pocket. "Don't worry about a thing," he told her.

Chapter Twelve

The telethon was a fiasco.

Dennis Devlin stood before the cameras throughout the long night, marshaling a parade of nonentities, promising viewers repeatedly "a planeload of stars from New York and Hollywood are en route and due any moment."

There was martial music galore. Twenty-three high school bands were assembled in the police-barricaded block adjoining the stage door, a Prussian nightmare of uniforms for Urban Giles. An abundance of tap dancers, accordionists and local Sinatras also populated the spotlights during the lengthy prologue to disaster.

Lederer, reporting from exile, had given him a last-minute rise of hope with his assurance that everything had been arranged irrevocably prior to his exit from the firm; that all the stars promised had made verbal commitments to him which he was certain they would honor. But it was a piece of blue sky which clouded rapidly. About midnight, Urban frantically checked all the major airlines and chartering firms in New York. None of them knew of any contingent of stars headed for Toledo. None of them even knew of any celebrities whatsoever aboard any of their Toledo flights.

Panic finally progressed to numbness, reviving as controlled fear. Rows of telephone operators, most of them volunteers, sat gossiping offstage, their instruments silent after the initial few hours. He threw Lisa Scott and Betty Chaplin before the cameras with the most appealing disease victims available, abandoning his own carefully paced programming schedule in a desperate effort to stimulate contributions and keep the show alive.

Elliot Ruskin stood oaklike in the forest of cameras and lighting equipment, shaking his head over and over, unable to verbally communicate his complete dismay to Giles. Fortunately for Urban, even a fiasco required him everywhere at once, keeping him a moving target, avoiding any prolonged confrontations with board members, or union officials, or disillusioned volunteers. He was aware somehow of not having seen Ruth Fuller at any time during the day of final preparation nor on telethon eve. If she was stalking him, as he imagined, he would have preferred to have her within his range of vision.

"I just checked the rating service you hired," Clarice whispered as he paused momentarily. "We're down from a forty-two point nine sampling at the opening to twenty-one point seven a few minutes ago."

He flared at her, as though she were responsible for the count. "It's just an area outfit. What the hell do they know?"

"We're not even making expenses so far, Urb. And we're heading into the dead hours."

He placed an elbow in one hand, the other arm striped diagonally across his chest, its hand cupping his chin. "Listen, Clare," he said, barely moving his lips behind the mask of fingers. "As soon as you can, slip the kids out of here, check out of the hotel and take a cab to Detroit airport——"

"Oh, God, Urb."

"Wipe that startled look off your face. Everybody's watching us as it is."

"We'll never get away with it. We can't just run."

"There's no alternative. We've still got a few thousand. By morning they'll have that and me and the house and the business."

She was suddenly sympathetic to his dilemma—to *their* dilemma. "Detroit airport? Not Toledo?"

"Detroit. Wait for me there in a motel. Whichever one's closest to the airport." He paused. "Use your maiden name when you register."

She looked at him as though it could be the last time. Running away held enormous legal implications in a business sense, but none of them mattered to her at the moment. "Will you take the car?"

He nodded calmly. "I'll leave it at the airport."

"Urb——"

"Better get moving. It's all uphill from here on."

"Good luck," she said.

It was strange, a bizarre remoteness to it, witnessing his own telethon in progress on the motel television set. It was even stranger leaving it shortly after, fluttering and gasping in its final hours, to board a flight to New York. He wondered if viewers—that was assuming there were still any left—could read what he read so clearly on the faces of the professionals he had hired. What happened to Giles? Where the hell is Giles? The possibility of his escape, his total escape and not just a fadeout into the nearest bar, would not yet have crossed their consciousnesses, much less have joined their list of likely probabilities. They were engaged right now in searching neighborhood saloons— he was certain of that—convinced the mounting debacle had driven him to break his pledge of sobriety until the last pledge was tallied.

He drank to that abandoned pledge from his own silver flask, a gift to himself from himself only the day before. He had been through too many prior productions not to sniff disaster all over the Toledo scene weeks before, beginning with Lederer, whose exodus from Whitcomb and Wiley had merely been an anticipated *coup de grace*.

"Want a little?" He extended the gleaming cap to Clarice in the seat next to him.

"I wish you wouldn't," she said.

"Don't worry about a thing," he laughed with just a touch of hysteria fringing it.

Thank God it was a weekend. They would be free of any court injunctions, subpoenas or whatever the fates now were preparing for them. After they said that, there was little else to say. Everything else had been said and said and said. The past was dead. The present was dead. They were not yet ready to begin discussing the future.

"Will we start school right away?" Maria wondered. Clarice had impulsively bought her a white dress in an airport boutique a few hours before. She looked flower-fresh and pretty in it as she stood in the aisle next to them.

"I'm not sure. I think school has started in the East."

"Ugh," Ramon grunted.

They accepted the hurried transitions of their lives with the complacency of youth accustomed to mobility. There was always a spirit of adventure in any change of environment, even returning to a familiar one after being away. Urban had even hinted vaguely they might not remain for long in Elmhill.

"Will we go back to the lake next summer?" Maria asked.

"Maybe," he said.

"I hope so. I like it there."

"We'll see," Clarice added. "Next summer's a long way off."

"Ruth wants us back," Ramon said.

"We'll see," she repeated.

By the time they landed at La Guardia, the flask was empty. But his mind was full. He knew for the first time in many months exactly what had to be done next.

Book Two

Chapter Thirteen

Nothing so rattled the transplanted, northern-bred psyche in Los Angeles as its synthetic portrayal of winter holidays. Christmas in particular. Wilshire Boulevard simply was not Fifth Avenue no matter how many green garlands were strung from streetlamps, no matter how many Santas stood decorating its corners in summer-weight suits of red and white.

Still, Urban Giles had reason to revel in the confetti snow of the department store displays, in the counterfeit trappings of fake fireplaces, stuffed reindeer and make-believe sleighs. He was at-large in a sense, but freely so. The family was comfortably settled in a rented house in the Hollywood Hills, no process servers had as yet haunted its doorstep, the children were reasonably content with their new school, the litter of foul publicity was thousands of miles to the east of him, a distant and now uninhabitable beach strewn with the past. He would never return. Perhaps it was that realization which touched this particular replay of the holidays with a special nostalgia and made him resent its artificiality.

In spite of his thoughts, he threw a crumpled dollar into the kettle of a Salvation Army bell ringer—his only charitable donation of the year despite the hundreds he claimed annually on his income-tax statements. It was a unique tribute to the organization that he regarded General William Booth's uniformed legions as the only reputable outfit in the charity business.

"God bless you," the girl said.

There were no winter winds to bend into, so he simply looked away into the sharp sun and quickened his stride. Gratitude disturbed him because he doubted its authenticity. There was little for him to be speeding to—only a cubicle in a professional office space and answering service setup—but he had not yet tamed his New York pace.

"Urban Giles!" a voice called out cheerfully. He reacted like a trapped animal, not certain whether to attempt escape or await his fate in the hope of mercy from the hunter. The Hemingwayesque beard, the elongated sideburns he now wore had not fooled at least one person.

"Dammit, I thought that was you! All done up in disguise. How the hell are you? And the children?"

He lifted his eyes and met those of Keith Avery, the adoption attorney. Relief was almost visible for a moment, he was certain, but he quickly retreated to a more guarded posture. "Well, well. Hello, Keith. Happy holidays."

"What are you doing here? Off on some secret mission for the Heart Fund or something?" he asked genially.

Should he tell him of his move? Or should he play along with the vacation-visit idea? Fabricating with an attorney so intimately involved with his past could only lead to detection and embarrassment, he decided.

"Didn't you know? We moved out here a few months ago."

"Hey, I'm a lawyer, not a detective. How would I know?"

"The kids just couldn't take the eastern winter," he lied.

"Oh? That cold already out there?"

He balked and recovered. "Well, not really, Keith. But when they start shivering in September, you know they've got California blood."

They joined in a brief laugh. "What are you up to out here? Got anything good going?"

Urban fished out a card, impressively embossed, its center line reading: COUNCIL OF COMMUNITY CONCERN. URBAN GILES, PRESIDENT. He had always believed in opulent stationery and business cards as devices for conning the lay public. But Keith Avery was no layman in the art of striking professional postures. He regarded its transparency with curiosity but did not comment on it.

"Where are you living?"

"The Hills."

"Beverly?"

"No," Urban said, smiling. "Hollywood."

"Write down the address on the back of your card," he said. He returned it to him with his pen. "I'd like to talk to you about something."

There it was again, Urban thought. It was still working. He could feel the spark leap, like static electricity, from one calculating mind to another. It ignited new hope in him all at once, as though he had been reconnected to the game board and given another chance to play.

"I'd like that, Keith. I have a great deal of respect for you."

A serrated smile cut across Avery's mouth. "Good to see you, Urb," he said, hand extended. "You'll hear from me. In the meantime, happy holidays and my best to the family."

They shook hands briefly and then he was gone, inserted into the moving garden of shoppers. Urban turned around impulsively and went back to the same Salvation Army girl, dropping a five-dollar bill into the kettle this time.

"A very Merry Christmas to you, sir," she said.

"Same to you," he replied. Strangely, for the first time in years, he actually meant it.

They spent the holiday in comparative isolation, surrounding a collapsible plastic tree with gifts he had purchased on his trips downtown. There was only one car between them, leaving the responsibility of shopping mostly to him.

Clare disliked journeying any distance from the house. The Toledo disaster had robbed her of much incentive; what little remained she directed toward the children. She had concluded, in long private seances with herself, that she was not truly a hedonist. Slightly more so, perhaps, than the people she passed in the supermarket four blocks down the hill, but not much more. What did make her different, what separated her in the filtering of personality types, was that she had consented to wander from the established norm. It did not matter that she had done so initially at the prodding of her husband. Nor did it matter, she supposed, that she possessed truly maternal instincts running parallel to her sexual drives. Surely, she enjoyed the physical services of a young body, with its taut muscle structure where most older men presented only flab and dilation. But it was not paramount in her life. She could take it or leave it. Moving among her own generation, her own gender, she was convinced now the majority of them in similar circumstances would have decimated the boy without concern for either his present or his future. It made her happier about herself to be thinking this way and she was determined to continue it.

"What are these red things? Apples?" Ramon held two of them aloft, selected from piles of them strewn about the base of a tree.

"Pomegranates," Urban said. "You should know that, Ray. They're California fruit."

"I only know apples and oranges."

"Try one."

"How?"

"Break it open. But watch out for the juice. It'll squirt like a grapefruit."

All of them watched as Ramon dug his thumbs into the blushing grenade. It fell partially open, a streak of fluid striking his eye.

"Good," Urban said. "Now you know. Eat that reddish purple part and you'll have a thousand children."

Maria giggled and began opening one of them herself. Soon all of them were dismembering pomegranates. Mixed reactions resulted from the contents. As they toiled over them, Urban dipped frequently into a huge rented punchbowl, passing cups to Clarice at intervals. They had discovered early the totality of rented life in California. Nothing had to be purchased. Literally everything was rentable.

The children—Clarice continued to insist on referring to them as such—were given unlimited license to the soda deposits in the refrigerator on Christmas Eve. They invaded them with abandon. On the color television—rented—they watched the ice skaters at Rockefeller Center, followed by the Mormon Tabernacle Choir singing carols in Salt Lake City. There were local scenes, too, but Urban insisted on rejecting them as artificial. All in all, it was a good night, for a change, filled with *gemutlichkeit*. That was largely due to the parents' avoidance of areas of conflict in their lazy conversations.

"Open your presents," Urban said about ten P.M. Neither Maria nor Ramon was acquainted with Yule procedure.

"The boxes?" Maria asked.

"Those with your name on them are yours," he said.

They were delighted with their gifts, dolls for her, slot cars for him, bicycles for both of them. The laugh of the evening was Urban's gift to Clarice, a device called a breast-rest. It consisted of two hollows in a polyfoam wedge, the instructions stating to insert the bosom "for restful, prone sleeping for women of all dimensions." Maria insisted on trying it. "It feels good," she declared.

It was remarkable how swiftly all of them had made the transition to their new lives. Urban reflected on that later as he continued his dipping into the punchbowl. The new promise of Keith Avery had strengthened him again, enabling him to look back over his shoulder for the first time since their arrival in California.

Red tapers danced upward as he peered into the revolving replica of a log. They licked at the ceiling and drew jagged lacerations across his face. He had told Clarice just about everything he had thought or done in his adult life. Perhaps with a few minor exceptions. What husband dared confide to his wife sexual aspirations that extended beyond her, beyond her own abilities? Yet, somehow he could not tell her what had happened to the old house in Elmhill. They had loved it and its seclusion, its history and stability in a life of insecurity and ceaseless change. Now it was gone forever.

The loss had accomplished something, however. It had reunited them again. Permanently. They slept in the same room again, in the same bed, as much for succor as sex. Survival's primacy among drives had, at least for a time, supplanted many earlier notions. She wanted to believe that, and he tried, even convincing himself of it occasionally.

She sat next to him after the children were upstairs in bed, peering absently with him into the make-believe fire. "Christmas would have been beautiful in Elmhill, wouldn't it?" she mused. He had entered a dreamy state, induced by the hour and the punchbowl. "That was such a strange fire, Urb, wasn't it? You know, the way it sprang up in different places around the house——?"

"I thought we were going to forget about it, Clare.

Don't spoil Christmas. The insurance investigators said the timbers were simply dried out after two centuries. It makes sense. . . ."

"I know. But how did it start? That's what bothers me."

"Come on now, stop it. We're lucky we got the insurance money so fast." He sank his cup into the dwindling sea of toddy without bothering to use the ladle. "In a way, you know, that fire was our lucky break. By now, the Toledo crowd would have had so many injunctions against the property, we'd never get any of it."

She sighed and sipped from the cup he had filled for her, this time with the ladle. "I'm just glad we were all away when it happened. Suppose the children had been there by themselves?"

He had wondered incessantly since that night whether she suspected him. The project had required an elaborate series of alibis and quick movements from place to place to divert any suspicion of arson away from him. Fortunately, the local fire department was a volunteer outfit. They had not even entertained a vague suspicion of any deliberate setting, particularly since it was of such irreplaceable historic value. It had gone up with unexpected swiftness, leaping the stone fixtures like hurdles in a race against time. The scent of smoke had forced him to bury his clothes several miles away. He returned to the family in different clothes from those in which he had left. It was the single clue he had not anticipated and eliminated. It was the one he thought she might have detected. They were at a Poconos mountain lodge on a weekend vacation after the strain of the telethon—logical, wasn't it?—when word came to them via the Pennsylvania State Police. The police were most helpful and sympathetic, even providing them with an escort over much of the distance. And even the most indignant of the Toledo victims called a sabbatical in legal moves until family matters could be organized after the tragedy. Quick settlement of the insurance claim had enabled them to vanish almost overnight. It was still a big country and Urban Giles was still just one individual within it.

He stroked his new beard thoughtfully. Because of the children, because of his professional credentials and old but important letters of recommendation, he could not extend his disguise to his name. That would have made his dropout complete. But Los Angeles was a city one could get lost in. Everyone was a stranger to everyone else. Still, the chance meeting with Keith Avery had rather refuted that. Perhaps that was why he was not one hundred percent contented on this Christmas.

"The bikes went over best of all," she said.

He left his reverie. "Yes. I should have gotten you one, too."

She laughed softly. "You got me a Bosom-Buddy."

"Is that what it's called?"

"Trademark registered." She threw the pillowlike object over to him.

"Did you see Maria? She's filling out fast. She could use one of these herself."

"Urb? Why don't we stop it now? Now that we're in a new house and all."

He licked the toddy from his lips and put the glass

aside. "Come on," he said. "Let's go to bed. We're all getting a little tired."

It was fortunate that Keith Avery did not read television trade journals. Stories on the Toledo fiasco, plus subsequent followups of union actions, General Aid Fund suits for breach-of-contract, and sweeping indictments on the entire telethon concept pioneered by Urban Giles Associates peppered their pages for weeks. An editorial in one of them, *Telly Visions,* called for grand jury action "against the naked frauds perpetrated by Urban Giles Associates in the name of charity." Floyd Jasper was enjoying a free-lance field day selling articles on the subject from his extensive files.

But adoption attorneys, even those with filmland ties, did not often peruse entertainment trade papers. And, as it turned out, it would not have mattered much to Avery anyhow. He could appreciate the rogue in any man clever enough to commit indiscretions without landing in jail.

"Here's what I have in mind," he proposed coolly over lunch. "You're basically a fund raiser, right?" He continued without awaiting a response. "I know from personal experience that there's an enormous market and an enormous need for homes to assist unwed pregnant girls who don't want abortions. I know because it's a kind of legal specialty of mine—putting adoptive parents in touch with girls who want to give up their babies for social or economic reasons. . . . But you're aware of that already, aren't you, Urban?"

He shook his head until Avery leaned into it, eclipsing his face with his own profile. "There's a fortune in it," he said. "And it's legitimate all the way."

"Do you want to set up a boiler room?"

"You tell me. I want to solicit donations."

"Fund raising. That's what it is basically. But hard sell. Fast. With real heat on the donors."

"I'm listening."

Urban expanded easily with the relaxed pressure. "We could put a dozen or so good men on the phones," he said. "All we need are the lines and maybe a loft somewhere. Centrally located. You need pickup men out here. No subways and buses like New York. . . ."

"Go on. I like what you're saying."

"Radio cars would be perfect. You've got to get the money while the pitch is hot—before they can talk it over with somebody or reconsider. The cars get cued in right from the boiler room. They pick up the money before the words even have time to fade away."

Avery touched Urban's sleeve. "I like it, Urb," he said.

They parted an hour later with much of the deal set. Avery would stake the operation at the beginning, reverting to silent partner with Urban after initial investment expenses were recovered. Meanwhile, Urban was to draw three hundred a week in addition to operational costs. It was a small beginning, but large for the locale. And when his own severed status was considered, it was a bonanza for Urban. He reported home that night with restored vitality, his ego loose and ready to roam again.

Her young body, like a fresh sponge, seemed to absorb him as he lay damp against it. Clarice and Ramon were gone—off to Farmers' Market on a long-postponed shopping expedition—leaving him free to indulge the revival of his fantasies. This time he knew he had not fooled his wife. But this time it did not matter.

"Sit up here on my chest," he told Maria, separating her legs as though making a wish. It was remarkable how much it did resemble the face of a cat. "I love your little pussy," he said. Her thighs were soft as melted candles against his face. He rubbed the nap of his sideburns against them, imagining he was transmitting a luxuriance she could feel.

"What should I do now?" he asked. He had taught her the lines and she knew them well now.

"Suck my pussy," she said.

He dove into the coral shell, a faint trace of mussels and seaweed flavoring it, losing himself in the delicate ripples of flesh, parting them first with his fingers and then his tongue, thriving on the rush of blood to his cock which was pointing at her from behind, lathered with excitement, a collection of white foam gathered at its tip.

She threw herself backward after a time, angled away from his insistent tongue, only inches above the rise of his cock. "I'm going to come," she gasped, uprooting him with her words, stroking him violently until he burst, spitting runny white pellets against the bottom of her face.

"Ugh," she said when both of them had died down.

"What, dear?"

"It's just like snot from my nose," she said, blotting beneath her chin with a handful of tissues.

They were becoming like a married couple, he thought. At least after, if not before.

There could be no further telethon projects under the aegis of Urban Giles—at least not in the foreseeable future. Not that he particularly cared now. His name was on the "unfair" list of all the key theatrical unions—from the American Federation of Musicians to the American Guild of Variety Artists—and the necessary settlements involved many more thousands of dollars than he cared to invest, or, more exactly, *could* invest, in restoring himself to acceptability.

He kept himself current on developments by reading *The Hollywood Reporter* and *Daily Variety,* plus doing a bit of research in their back-issue files. The result was a small but telling diary of his collapse as a television entrepreneur. Most of the stories had trickled off into occasional one-liners by now. It was, after all, relatively small potatoes in the vast stew of show business and hardly warranted detailed follow-up after the first flurry of reports. The novelty was over, and no business tired more quickly of its own indiscretions. It was not so much a case of forgive and forget as it was simply *forget*. The litter of discarded careers was everywhere.

One small item did peak in his radarlike scrutiny. It was datelined Toledo and stated succinctly:

Elliot Ruskin, president pro tem of the General Aid Fund board of directors which sponsored the disastrous telethon of Sept. 15 here, was defeated in his bid for a full term in office by a unanimous vote. Newly named to the post was Matthew Boylan, local publisher. Estimates of losses to the Fund as a result of the TV debacle and resulting cancellations of pledges now total upward of $600,000.

He was relieved to find no further mention of UGA in the paragraph. Threatened lawsuits had probably diminished by now, he hoped. The legal grounds were actually quite flimsy as he saw them.

There was considerable validity in his contention, whether he fully realized it or not. He *had* organized a major telethon as contracted for. No celebrities were mentioned in the official document. That part of it had been done verbally, a poor legal area but Urban Giles's most potent area of achievement.

He actually enjoyed setting up the boiler room for Avery. The best fund raisers in the game were mostly alcoholics, with a few soft drug addicts among them. A man had to be a drinker, or diluting his senses in some other way, to stomach the distasteful raping of another man's finer civilized sensibilities, sentiment and charity.

Urban moved among the element easily, somehow achieving a sense of superiority for himself in the process.

"Here's the pitch," he briefed the first covey of candidates. "We're backed by outstanding civic leaders —no names, though—and we're meeting a desperate need to save our community's children from lives of despair, drug addiction and child abuse. . . ." He paused, his gaze circling the room like a lariat, capturing the essence of the crop. They looked good—

intelligent, alert and dissipated. "The concept is spelled out in the folders on the table before you. I want you to take them home with you, study them thoroughly, and report back here tomorrow for a follow-up briefing." He hesitated. "Now, you're all invited to join me for a get-acquainted drink in the cocktail lounge directly across the street." Applause greeted his closing remark.

Later that night, his optimism widened, quadrupled by four martinis, he escorted Keith on a tour of the setup. It was basically one long, rectangular room with several rows of tables dividing it, dozens of telephones and wooden boxes strewn about them. There was a private office for Urban at the near end, permitting him to view the entire operation any time he opened his door. It was an essential precaution, considering the errant natures of typical employees in the business. They were all transients, all inconsistent, all masochistic, he explained.

"What are the boxes for?" Avery asked.

"Look inside. They're soundproofed. When a man has a fish on the line, he ducks inside. It gives the pitch an aura of privacy, even intimacy the way some of these guys lay it on. . . ."

"Hey. Simple but effective."

"If you see the place when it's really rolling, you'll know why it's called a boiler room."

"Loud, huh?"

"It'd be easier to sleep in a real one."

Avery nodded his head approvingly. "Looks good."

"Wait till you see the money roll in," Urban said.

Chapter Fourteen

Inconsistency being the long-accepted prerogative of her gender, Clarice Giles picked up her option on it, exercising it without embarrassment or explanation. The return of a money flow to their lives was almost intravenous in the directness of its stimulation. It effectively ended her brief flirtation with her old concept of morality.

"Where do you disappear all the time with that bike?" she quizzed Ramon late one afternoon.

"Up the hill."

"There are lots of hills around here. Besides, what do you do all that time—wherever it is?"

"Nothing."

She had been padding about the house all afternoon in housecoat and slippers, simmering quietly, enjoying the ginger-ale bubbling of her bloodstream, mentally mixing the ingredients she imagined would blend best with her reactivated chemistry.

"Maria says you have a girlfriend." It was just a ruse, but just such ruses had flushed the truth from many people through history.

"She's a liar."

"Come on, Ramon. There's nothing wrong with having a girlfriend, is there?" She ran her fingers into his hair, tousling it, teasing him.

"She's got a boyfriend. That's why she lied."

Her face opened to the illumination. "Oh? Is that where she goes all the time, too?"

"He walks her home every day."

"Well, she's getting to be a big girl, isn't she?"

"They say bad things about her." His anger at the accusation had unhinged the lock on his secrets regarding her.

"What do they say, Ramon?"

He looked away, as though his words would become visible and he did not want to see them. "She's fucking," he said.

Clarice could not explain the strange immunity the revelation gave her, nor the release of sexual adrenalin it inspired within herself. Somehow it pleased her when it should have displeased her and she felt the need to convey that reversed reaction to him.

"It's probably just jealousy that makes them say such things," she said comfortingly, drawing him to her. "Maria's a pretty little girl and lots of boys would like to do that to her." She slipped one of her hands under his shirt and rubbed the smooth expanse of his back. "Besides, it's a very nice thing to do when you do it with someone you love."

At his age, even skirting the subject of sexuality was sufficient to build an erection. She resisted the desire to grab it immediately, angling herself instead so that it almost caught in a pocket of her coat. Her breasts pushed into his chest like huge marshmallows.

"You like to fuck, don't you, Ramon?" she whispered. Youth was making another of its infrequent encores within her. It was summer in her soul once more and she closed her eyes to insure its capture. I am desirable, she thought. And in truth she was put together rather well, according to the numbers, her nose middled, eyes evenly centered and proportioned, mouth underlining mathematically, chin cupping properly below, perhaps to catch the fall which had begun, still reasonably solid but threatening to avalanche in the not too distant future. Her tits were her pride, her chief attraction, and like any woman beginning a slide, she clung to them, coveted them, exploited them as her treasures. They rose above him now, there on the carpeted floor, her body looming beyond them, all of it a massive extension of his cock, sandwiched into the wet valley below.

She slowed her furious opening pace to reach behind him, fingering the hole behind his balls in counter-rhythm to her own undulations. He was beneath her, a trapped victim, a look of almost primitive submission printed over his face.

"You should fuck girls now," she said to excite herself, releasing the words between shallow gasps, as though they came relayed from the mouth below because it could not speak for itself. "While your prick is still so hot and beautiful."

"Yes," he said.

"You can bring them here. I want you to do it here. I want to see you do it. I want to see you fuck." Her upbringing gave the word a wicked connotation no matter how often she employed it, increasing the pleasure of its emergence from her. "Will you do that for me?"

"Yes."

At that she clutched his cock tightly, feeling its tension, its mounting desire to spurt. She raised herself slightly to brush the head of it against her top rim, stroking it fully as she did. The combination of everything brought a unison response, thick drops of rain falling into her forest, flashes of lightning storming her, and she fell upon him in a wet mass.

It was there on the floor, still damp with sweat and the syrup of lovemaking, that Maria found them.

Urban Giles was functioning on two levels in his revived life, one elevated, the other subterranean. He attempted to pull them into a closer parallel, but in doing so he risked lowering the upper more than he stood a chance of lifting the lower. It frustrated him at a stage of his life when he needed all elements lofted to maintain a sense of balance and direction.

On the bright side, he thrived on the new permissiveness of his setup with Avery. Like a fish who had solved the intricacy of a net entrapping him, he was back swimming in the open sea, free to go off in all directions, gills intact. Keith had carefully shrouded the operation in legal whole cloth, the money was good, and he was in more or less absolute control. No problems there. At least not as yet.

On the dark side, he was melancholy over his own diminished potency. It was a problem so intimately personal he could not discuss it even with Clarice. The old paranoia was returning in this area. He imagined even shyly sensual little Maria secretly laughed at his obvious decline in just the short time they had been together as father and daughter, lover and loved. It was silly—ridiculous—he told himself intermittently, in the moments of chill sobriety interrupting his diligently maintained intoxication. But it would not leave him, clinging to the edges of him even in the most intense light. Clinically, he was distressed over the runny quality of his ejaculations, the single jolt they now gave him as opposed to the series of orgasms he had experienced in the past, the way the fluid escaped him in a slow, almost reluctant cascade, barely clearing the rim of his crown, never reaching for the stars as it had. He had not lost his sense of humor in most respects, but some of his perceptiveness, some of his insouciance in matters of libido, were faltering and he sought now to bolster them with a new bravado.

Clarice reported Maria's discovery of her with Ramon, describing it in terms of parental concern rather than the libertine language he was seeking. "I want to be aroused, not depressed," he complained. There was always this conflict, this mix of emotions for her. But she did understand his need for verbal graphics and she was accustomed to his self-stimulating commentary.

"Ramon says the kids at school talk about her. They say she's playing around with boys. He even said *fucking*."

"That's what it's called, isn't it? Kids should get all the fucking they can while they're young."

"No, Urb. A girl's got to be careful."

"She can't wear it out. It stretches."

"She's too young to get a reputation like that."

"Know something? I'm glad to hear it. It's the best thing for her to pass it around. It'll keep her from becoming one of those one-dimensional women who fall in love with every guy who lays them. Or they can't come unless they're in love."

"I wouldn't mind so much if she brought them home. I'd feel better about it then."

He laughed. "Maybe catch a little for yourself that way?"

"I told Ramon to bring his girls here. I want to make sure he goes out with nice girls."

He laughed again. "I'll check those out myself. I'm just as concerned a parent as the next guy."

"Kids talk. That worries me all the time."

"The secret, my dear, is to get them involved so anything they say could implicate them." His beard wrote broad strokes in the air. The hair in it was almost pubic in quality, bristly but resilient, curled tightly and lighter in color than the hair of his head.

"It's all dangerous."

"Isn't everything? Hasn't it always been?"

There were sequins in his eyes now. She had opened up a whole new corridor of contemplation for him. He sat sipping from his glass, eyes distant, mind conjuring.

"I'd like to give a little party," he said. "A little, get-acquainted, housewarming kind of thing for some of their little friends." He did not seek her opinion. His pants had risen in acclamation. It was the only vote that counted.

As a dealer in children, a negotiator with young mothers, Keith Avery had developed a kind of sixth sense about people, particularly those with parental aspirations. There was a facet of Urban Giles he had not yet examined and solved and, as he became more familiar with him, the curiosity factor enlarged and crowded a corner of his mind. He left it there, fermenting, until finally he decided it was time to sample the mystery ingredient.

"The kids must really be growing by now," he said casually over cocktails. "I'd like to see them sometime."

Urban listened to the overture without reaction showing. "Sure," he said. "Why not?"

"Nothing official or anything like that, Urb," he added hastily. "I just like to follow up on my placements. Make sure they're happy, that sort of thing. I'm sure they love you and Clarice."

"You know how kids are. Sometimes yes, sometimes no."

"Like women?" He laughed lightly. "I know what you mean. But keep it in mind. Some weekend, maybe."

"I will."

"Now, about the program," he shifted gears smoothly. "I envision a series of cottage-style communities for girls who are in trouble, or just alone and pregnant, a kind of place where they can spend the final weeks before giving birth in a cheerful, optimistic environment, somewhere that'll strengthen and encourage them for the difficult role of giving birth and then giving up their children."

"I know, Keith. I know just what you mean. In fact, I wrote part of that pitch, remember?"

Keith smiled tentatively. "I got carried away. Maybe I should stick my head into one of those boiler room boxes and start selling pledges myself."

Urban signaled the waitress for another round.

"First, you'll have to learn to drink faster. Boiler rooms run on booze."

When they parted, Avery threw in another seemingly casual mention of visiting the children. It was precisely the kind of casual signal which the Giles radar picked up immediately, alerting him to potential danger. He went home from their meeting and lay awake for what seemed hours, brooding over it, before sleep finally filed it away until morning.

Chapter Fifteen

One day was like every other in the matter of spectrum. First it yellowed, then oranged, blued and returned to blackness. But colorations were not the sum total of any day, particularly when they were the constants and people the variables.

Urban sought solace away from the hysteria of his headquarters this late afternoon, the blue-orange part of it, turning into one of the bars on a street spidering off Hollywood Boulevard. It was the kind of place where men drank beer directly from bottles and "fuck" served interchangeably as a noun, verb and adjective. The bartender sized him up obliquely when he ordered a martini, gathering the materials for it as though his request was an imposition.

He didn't care about the man's reaction, turning from it to stare vacantly at the banked fire of sunset reflecting against the window. The charity pitch was going beautifully, particularly the inspired radio patrol to facilitate pickups of pledges. People had a way of fluctuating in their generosities. The time to get the money, as he had told Keith, was as soon after their commitment as possible—while they were still convinced of the nobility of purpose aroused in them by the boiler-room phone men, before embarrassment over a change of heart could solidify their resolve to renege on the verbal pledge. Hardly five minutes elapsed with the radio cars, resulting in close to ninety-percent collections. Compared with the usual fifty-five percent or less on delayed follow-ups, the cost of the cars had proved a very small investment. "You're a damn genius," Keith had said when he read the reports. After three martinis, the title struck him funny and he laughed aloud at his recollection of it.

"Drink up, buddy," the bartender said. He gathered up the napkin and swizzle stick before him, his blunt hands in readiness as he waited for the glass.

"What for?"

"You've had enough, that's what for."

"You're kidding." It was coldly obvious he was not, but he said it anyhow, a cliche uttered to fit a stock situation. He had seen it happen often to others. Until now it had never happened to him.

The bartender made the loop around the end of the bar in a single swoop, his thick fingers digging into the fabric of Urban's jacket, ripping him from the stool. "Git the fuck outta here," he said menacingly, pushing him toward the door. In that instant, all the colors of the day ran together, the palette smashed and splintered as he ground it into the mountain about to avalanche upon him.

"He's stabbin' Frankie!" someone shouted, the voice seeming to come down a hollow corridor to reach him. It was all so crazy, so bizarre and remote, and he stared at his hand with detachment, wondering at the ripe red pulp oozing from it, trying to assemble again, so abruptly, the jagged edges of the puzzle that was his life. Claustrophobia seized him as the faces slid down the long alley of the bar room, like bowling balls bent on knocking down the pins of him. Instinctively, a quadruped again after all the centuries, he bolted for the door, pushing it open with his head, an animal escaping from his cage, his wounded hand inserted into the pouch of his jacket, dashing headlong with the baying hounds in pursuit, shouts of "Police!" and "Stop him!" puncturing the violet dusk. He ran his frenzied race into unfamiliar bits and pieces of streets and backyards, scrambling up the steep rise of terrain, terracing it with flying feet, his lungs sucking the evening air in wild gasps until finally he collapsed, cowering, into the dark pocket of a strange garage dug into the hillside.

There was no way of telling how long he lay there, sick with fear and exhaustion, feeling the sharp pain in his hand now that escape was no longer the foremost concern. Gradually, he was able to assemble a probable if not positive explanation of what had happened to him in those kaleidoscopic moments. He had apparently thrust the stem of the martini glass into the bartender as they scuffled, shattering it in his own hand while piercing him. The blood had begun to jell across his palm now, caking on his fingers where it had been spread more lightly, smeared on his face like some Indian tribal design. It was all so ridiculous, so senseless, and yet life pivoted on just such absurdities. He did not aggravate himself, there in the dark, with an excess of whys and wherefores.

He made his way cautiously to the periphery of a business area, then edged into the rest room of a busy gas station. Behind the bolted door of a toilet, he rinsed his hand in the bowl, taking the risk of infection in preference to washing himself in full view of any man who might enter. The hand throbbed now, its ache pulsating with the beat of his heart. He could not bring himself to probe for the tiny glass splinters which seemed sprinkled throughout the wound, wrapping it instead in fragments of his shirt torn from the back and bottom. His face cleared easily, except of course for the eyes, meshed red and illuminated by an unerasable gleam of fright. With his left hand, he restored some order to his hair, brushed the bar room dust from his clothes and slipped swiftly out of the room and into the boulevard shadows. Pedestrian traffic was thin, as it always seemed to one accustomed to New York. He had no difficulty locating an empty telephone booth.

Clarice was near hysteria herself when she finally located his hiding place—an abandoned bus shelter miles from the scene of the altercation. She calmed sufficiently to perform the delicate surgery of removing the splinters of glass from his hand when they reached home. His only anesthesia was a bottle of gin, from which he sucked long and often.

In the morning, mind as numbed as hand, he slashed

off the incriminating beard. His parole was over. He was once more a fugitive.

With the basic pragmatism of her nature, Clarice moved to combat the ebb of security accompanying her husband's experience and his memory of it. The hand gradually regained its flexibility, the scar across its palm visible only when it was fully opened. It no longer represented a major problem, nor even a minor one. But Urban had been visibly shaken by the encounter, and once again in their stormy relationship she reluctantly but positively assumed control of the business. To speed his recovery—the psychic phase of it—she indulged his enlarged paranoia by allowing him to install mirrors throughout the house, particularly in their bedroom. He was comforted by their "protection"—enabling him to see around corners, over his shoulders, above and about him in every direction. If anyone was following him anywhere within his own castle, he was certain to know about it.

The mirrors soon suggested an even more promising prospect for enlightened mental rehabilitation. He went into the office with Clarice each morning, but he returned home before her to await the children's arrival from school. In the wheaty light of a late afternoon, his vision transported in relays from mirror to mirror, he saw Maria pull aside her jumper, lower the pink elastic of her panties and toy with herself; wetting her index finger, drawing an invisible circle on her lips, then dropping directly on target to the small root of her clitoris, teasing it as he imagined she would a small boy's penis.

His oblique viewing was electrified further by the

touches of paranoia flicking his moods. Practicing denial of a sort, he freed his bulging cock, only to see it multiply in the succession of mirrors, multiplying also the difficulty of restraint. She had begun to insert twin fingers into the folds where her body gathered, like velvet bunched in the clutch of Eros. He watched in fascination as she indulged her private self, seeking to quiet the hunger between her young legs. The freshness of her, the patina of innocence under which were hidden her much more sophisticated desires, drove him to her with an urgency no longer restrainable.

"Marialita," he said softly.

She looked up, startled, but the sight of him, flushed with aroused lust, erased her guilt. "You saw me in the mirrors," she said.

"You look nice that way."

His hands moved about her thighs, seeking to open the passage. She allowed him to bend her supple body to fit the angles of his own, settling readily into a sharp curve which projected the moons of her buttocks into the trajectory of him. Slowly, surely, he forced the swelling of himself into the warmth of her lower lips. In—out—in—out—in—out, timed by the metronome of his emotions, he drew upon the smooth syrup of her interior, the firm but gentle press of the walls gloving him, seeming to peel back the skin and then restore it.

"Look at us," he said. Their eyes glanced off one another, balls on a silver billiard table, and then another, and then another, black and steel marbles in silent collision all about them. He turned her as he would fine mahogany on a lathe, inviting her without words to study his workmanship as he advanced and retreated, a self-anointed craftsman in the art of lovemaking.

"When will we have our party?" she asked. He was pleased at her lifting of his thoughts, at her willingness to participate in verbal as well as physical games with him.

"Soon," he said.

"I told Helene. She wants to come. She keeps asking when."

Eyes upward, witnessing his penetration of her, he struggled to delay climax until more of the matter could be discussed, it's taste like fine wine in his mouth. "Who is Helene?" he asked.

"Don't you know? She has brown hair." Her abdomen contracted to the added hardness of him. "She has the big boobies. . . ."

The command to fire was out of his control. He erupted in a torrent, upstream in the crevice of her cheeks, a gray white gusher of inner oil spouting a fleur-de-lis above her spine, running over the sides of her like sugar icing on a cake. She had learned how to inspire an accompanying climax in herself, her fingers immediately resuming the manipulation in which he had discovered her, this time unnoticed by him in the aftermath of his own eruption.

Later, after they had showered and donned their pajamas, she asked again about the party. "Some other time," he said. The subject did not interest him any longer this day.

Inevitably, the past rose around him and sought to crush him. Ruth Fuller was in Los Angeles, she had conferred with Keith Avery, and she had intercepted

Ramon on his way home from school, a combination of circumstances which was at once malignant and contagious to all exposed to it.

"What's in it?" Keith asked directly.

"What did she say?" Urban countered.

"A whole raft of stuff about a telethon in Toledo."

"It's all passé."

"I agree with you. She left me a folder full of clippings. I'm not even going to look at them."

"Thanks, Keith."

Avery threw him a beveled look. "I'd like to see the kids. The sooner, the better."

He had just begun putting in full days at the office again, with Clarice replacing him in their new combination work cycle. She arrived with him mornings and left shortly after noon as he had been doing. The turnover in boiler room personnel was almost daily. None of them dealt in loyalties. They were like piece workers in a factory, paid according to their record of production. They cared little or nothing about their employers from one day to the next. Because of it, Urban was still uncertain of himself since returning full time and he wished somehow he could stall this request from Avery until that phase of his life evened out again.

"Could we make it a little later, Keith? I just got back and——"

"I'd like to do it today," he said firmly.

Urban stuck his finger into the empty zero hole of the telephone dial and drew quick arcs with it. There was no further exchange of conversation while they waited.

"Clare?" He knew it was her. The children were not

allowed to answer the phone. "I'm bringing Keith with me to see the kids." His face lengthened as he listened. "It has to be tonight. We'll see you in about two hours." He cradled the telephone carefully, deliberately.

"From what this woman said, you have a little Lolita on your hands," Keith said after the call.

Urban was uncertain what tack to take. "There are no tabs on her. She's not a paper doll, if that's what you mean."

"I don't think she should be."

They lapsed into wordlessness on the ride out. Only when he was in the vicinity of the house did they resume speaking. "Where do I go from here?" Keith asked.

"Right at the next intersection, then follow the road up the hill. Until you see Vista Lane."

"That's it?"

"No. But it's right off it a block or so."

Avery wound his way according to directions. "You know, the FBI couldn't find you up here."

Urban tried to laugh but couldn't.

Maria was waiting from them when they swung into the stub of driveway adjoining the garage. "That's her?" Avery asked.

"That's Maria."

"My God, she's another Raquel Welch."

Over him, all about him, surrounding him, imprisoning him, he heard the pitches breaking like fast curves. They were the dialogue of his furtive occupation and he functioned among them with the stubborn efficiency of a bullpen catcher, ignoring some, fielding others, shouting encouragement to the faltering, doling out speedy rewards to the winners.

"Bill Seedman's in for three hundred," he barked from the doorway of his office. "Let's go, everybody! D-Day for the ducks!"

It was a sick business, preying as they did on the strained mercies of a populace already dunned to exhaustion by countless charities ranging from saving Alaskan seals to comforting impotent geriatric patients. Like a Greek chorus they chanted tragedy into the ears of the unwary or softly sympathetic, over and over the cries, their messages varying only slightly to fit the individual listener. Conversation spilled from them as freely as alcohol entered them, their voices like musical instruments, modulating with professional sensitivity to the mood and manner of each prospective donor. Away from the phones, they were a hard, cynical crew without the slightest spirit of camaraderie or compassion for one another.

"Shit," the woman before him said, her face a grape-purple, her eyes a hundred years older than her body. "I can't hustle a fuckin' dime with this pitch."

He did not know her name offhand, which made her no different from the others in the room, all of them bent like cartooned *nebbishes* into the silencing crates before them; grinning, frowning, gesturing into the blankness of the rectangle, selling themselves like heads of cabbage to unknown buyers at the other ends of the lines.

"You heard my announcement on Seedman," he said.

"Fuck him, too."

She was trembling ever so slightly and he dropped

his own hands below the desk level to hide their mild vibrato. A week was not enough time to adjust to the taut climate of the boiler room. "Tell you what, honey," he said. "I'll take you across the street and we'll have a little toast to Seedman."

"You got a buyer," she said without hesitation. She gathered herself together, smoothing the lines of her skirt, her teeth vising a cigarette. Urban decided she was the kind of woman who bet men in bars she could pick up a twenty with the lips of her snatch. And never lost.

"Tell me what's wrong with the pitch," he said to amuse himself across the street.

"It's not a woman's bag, that's all."

He leaned back and decided she was not so funny, after all. "You know something? You could be right."

"I know I'm right. Women don't buy that shit from other women. They want to hear it from men. Who's gonna believe some broad begging shelter for another broad?"

"Where'd you work last?"

"A vets' magazine. Ten bucks a year to show you care for our boys dying in Vietnam."

"That must be tough on percentages."

"Not bad. Six outta the ten."

He whistled. "That must really be a hustle."

"I'm a telephone solicitor, baby, cause I can't solicit my ass no more," she laughed. "That's our sorority song."

Keith Avery came through the door then, looked about and saw them.

"This is one of the girls on the team," Urban said, not bothering to find out her name.

"I figured. She's on the team medication."

"You want to see me?"

"If the lady will excuse us——"

"Fuck, no."

"Ah, *parlez vous Français?*"

Urban laughed as a torrent of invective spilled from the woman. They got up and left hurriedly.

"Dammit, Urb, you've got to be more selective in personnel," Avery said when they were outside.

"What's the matter? She's one of the finer specimens."

Avery slipped like a silver dagger into the sheath of his black Imperial. "Hop in," he said. "I want to introduce you to some *real* ladies."

Whatever he meant by that, Urban Giles was game. They were animals of the same species really, separated only by differences of environment at birth, raised according to different rules. Now thrown together by chance, they were living together parts of each day in the same cage in the same zoo, pacing off their distances cautiously, neither totally certain of the other, yet realizing a certain interdependence, even safety, in casting some lots together.

"Maria really is a Lolita," Avery said. He kept his eyes steadily on the freeway.

"She's a sweet girl."

"She seems very fond of both of you."

"It has worked out very well."

"Had any trouble with either of them?"

"None."

"Surprising. Really. Two kids like that, good-looking, right in the danger ages."

"Why danger?" He wanted the quiz to end, but it was not up to him to end it.

"Think she's still a virgin?"

Urban shifted uneasily. "That's a strange question to ask a father."

"Maybe you're right. You can take the Fifth on it if you like." His laugh following the comment was difficult to interpret.

"I think she knows what's going on, if that's what you mean."

"If she doesn't, Urb, the way she looks, then this generation of males is washed up."

They rode in silence for a while. Then Avery picked up more or less where he had left off. "You know, the older a man gets, the better the young stuff looks. Have you noticed?"

His mind froze. Was he being led into a trap? "I don't know. I haven't really thought about it."

"Hey, Urb, come on now. You only use glasses for reading. You mean you don't see all the young ones prancing around?"

"Well, yeah, of course I see them."

"And you don't get a little itch for it now and then? I know *I* do."

An old prosecution trick, Urban thought. Condescending to the level of the accused to wring a confession from him. "I'm older than you are, Keith."

"Next witness," he jested.

The boundary sign of Santa Monica flashed before them. Within minutes they were skirting the Pacific somewhere beyond Malibu. Abruptly, the car turned into a graveled area before a row of single-story, connected units. It resembled a motel in architecture.

"Let's go," Avery said. "I want you to see where some of the hard cash you're hustling is going."

It was an unexpected revelation for Urban. He had not really expected any of the money to actually be employed for the purpose for which it was being solicited, at least not so early in the operation. Perhaps he had been too hasty in his judgment of Keith's character and motivation. From his own experience, the skim-off in similar fund raisings seldom left enough for anything but bribes to investigators and the lavish brochures deemed necessary to depict projected facilities.

"This used to be a sharp little motel," Keith said as they approached the entrance. It confirmed Urban's first impression. "I used to come here a lot as a customer."

" 'PACIFIC PLACE,' " Urban read aloud from a small metal plate on the door.

"It's our first facility for young mothers-to-be. Eventually we'll have them all up and down the coast."

"Not bad. Not bad at all."

"Wait till you see the inside." He pushed the door open for him and held it. "Miss Gloria Renquist," he called out, dividing his voice to reach both Urban and the woman behind the registration desk, "this is Urban Giles, who's heading our fund-raising program."

"Mr. Giles," she responded, her body rising with her voice, "at last you've come to visit us at Pacific Place." She extended her hand over the partition. It hung there lifelessly until Urban could rescue it.

She was an odd assortment of woman—large-shouldered but small-breasted, her hair shorn close to her head, resembling a helmet more than a coiffure, dark-rimmed glasses dominating the triangle of her face, the overall effect more that of a muscular prison matron than of a professional social worker administering a modern, suburban refuge for wayward girls.

"Miss Renquist is the madam-in-charge," Avery said blithely. He was unusually flippant, an observation that did not escape Urban.

"Oh, Mr. Avery, you always say that. What is Mr. Giles going to think?"

"He'll think what a nice place we've got here. Right, Urb?"

"Right."

"We'll take a look around on our own, Gloria."

"A pleasure meeting you, Miss Renquist," Urban managed to utter before Keith turned him around a bend.

"The same," her voice angled after him.

"I'm going to introduce you to some of the residents," Keith whispered as they walked. "Just let me do the talking." They moved swiftly along the carpeted corridor, Avery walking through the hall as though it were part of his own home. Bypassing the first three doors, he tapped lightly on the fourth, pushing it open without waiting for a response. It was a neat, studio-styled room with a small kitchenette carved into the wall. A young girl stood warming something in a pan, hair spilling over her shoulders, halfway down her body. She was naked except for a heart-shaped apron knotted over her buttocks and extending in front to just below her other hair.

"Guess who?" Avery said. He had slipped up behind

her, cupping her breasts in his hands. The girl made no attempt to turn, continuing with her stirring.

"Where were you yesterday?" she asked.

"Busy."

"Where? Down the hall?"

He squeezed her nipples. "Ouch, god dammit," she said.

"What's that stuff you're making?"

"Vichyssoise."

"Potato soup."

"Sounds better my way."

"It's supposed to be cold, dearie."

"Give me a goddam chance, will you? I'm putting it in the refrigerator as soon as it cools off a little."

He stood up against her, the movement of her cheeks registering against his crotch. "Where'd you ever learn about vichyssoise, anyhow?"

"I used to be a waitress, remember? Before I discovered paradise on the Pacific." She laughed in a flute register, swinging free of him as she did so. It was the first awareness she had of Urban's presence. "Hi," she said nonchalantly.

"Glenny, this is Urban Giles. He's the man who's paying your rent."

"He is? I thought *you* were."

"Both of us are. In different ways."

She seemed disinterested.

"How about inviting Vicki over. I'd like her to meet Mr. Giles."

"No male guests. You know the rules."

"Get her."

She slipped out of the apron and shrouded herself

in a sheer negligee, curling out of the door like a puff of smoke.

"You'll like Vicki," Keith said. Urban kept quiet, as per instructions. "What would you like—Scotch, gin, brandy?" He was fingering an array of perfume bottles huddled on a small vanity table, all bearing the labels of expensive brands.

"Brandy, I guess. Or maybe a little Chanel Number Five."

The girls came in before Keith could counter his remark. "Where are all the glasses, Glen?"

"Use paper cups. You can take them out in your briefcase."

He spread the cups around, filling them partially from various bottles. "Introduce people, babydoll," he said.

"Vicki, this is Urban—is that right, Urban?"

"Yes, Urban. Hello, Vicki."

"That's a wild name," Glenny said.

Vicki was no more than seventeen or eighteen, with dark-rooted blonde hair and a bosom which pushed forcefully against the retaining wall of her brassiere. Her youth appealed to Urban immediately, overcoming his slight distaste for her premature pouchiness. Baby fat, he dismissed it, after checking the benefits of excess in her breasts.

"We're on an inspection tour," Keith announced straight-faced.

"I know what you're inspecting," Glenny said.

"How're the new girls?"

"Nothing special. Nothing you'd like."

He threw another splash of gin into his cup and

drained it. "Urban, the brandy's in the Joy decanter. Help yourself."

Questions brimmed all over Urban's mind, but he remembered Avery's warning and held them back.

"Did you bring any shit with you?" Glenny asked.

His face funneled. "I don't like that expression," he said. "You know the rules about drugs here."

She laughed mockingly. "I also know the rules on drinking and fucking."

Keith pulled her to himself and unhooked her gown, his hands following its descent along her body until he reached the rounded softness of her behind. "There's nothing about oral intercourse in any of the regulations," he said, kneeling before her. She wedged her fingers into his hair as he dug into her. "Clothes off, everybody," she said with a touch of resignation.

In less than a minute, they were all kittens and balls of yarn, pussies and cocks, arms and legs, tongues quivering, fingers probing, a montage of lubricated crevices and dark holes, perpendiculars and horizontals, angles and curves, a geometric happening vulcanized with reddened flesh and varnished with the special fluids of their sport.

Glenny removed the chianti head of Avery's cock from her mouth, pulling the skin from beneath it all the way up and over it, making a sheath, a helmet of tensed flesh, milking it until bubbling white foam gathered about its neck. "Anybody for vichyssoise?" she called out.

Vicki hung over Urban, her tits flopping loosely in his face, watching his entry into her. She was still observing when he climaxed, spurting cloudy dashes into the air.

By the time they departed almost two hours later, Urban had forgotten his questions, dispelled whatever doubts he had about everything, and thoroughly enjoyed his adventure in rest-home administration *à la* Avery. The girls were amazingly adaptable and uninhibited, almost professional, he thought.

"I've never told you this before, Urb," Keith said in the car, "but most of our girls have had experience as prostitutes. Some of them are even recommended to us from juvenile court."

They resumed the silence of their trip out on the return as well. Neither of them was in the mood for extended conversation after the strenuous party. Avery stopped the car at the foot of the hill where the Giles home was located.

"One thing more, Urban, before you go," he said softly. "I want to take Maria up the coast for a night."

Their eyes met and welded. There was no way for Urban to get away without answering. "All right," he said.

His last words of the day washed out all the others for both of them.

Chapter Sixteen

Sun, warm and generous, flooded the room. Maria purred like a mountain cat in its abundance. There was no school that day, but it had been necessary for both Urban and Clarice to report to the office, leaving the children to fend for themselves at least until noon.

"I love to do it in the morning," she said. "I wish we could sleep together all the time."

Their bodies lay naked on the rumpled sheets, like slender stones smoothed and polished by the sea and deposited on a white beach. She put her long fingers protectively over the soft shoot of flesh resting on his abdomen, her forefinger idly seeking the slotted entrance to it.

"Someday, they're gonna find out about us," Ramon said.

"I don't care. Nothing is wrong when two people love each other."

He saw the brief Latin flash of temper and it amused him. "You love a lot," he said.

She dug her finger nails into his penis. "I'll kill you someday," she said through frozen teeth. He knew better than to laugh at her when she was serious. But he could not hold down a smile.

She slapped him sharply, but without malice. "Hey, Maria, what do you call what you do then?" he began again.

"Loving and fucking are not the same."

He pinned her playfully against the sheets. "Now what should we do?"

"We love."

It was easy to see his act of taming her had aroused her rather than quieted her. Her body adjusted readily to the contours of bed and pillows, opening like a flower to his wand. She had grown to love the alternating secrecy and openness of their relationship, the conversations of their eyes, the tenderness of their dependence upon one another in the disconcerting climate of the Giles household. They had succeeded totally in masquerading the continuity of their affair. And obvious though it should have been, it had gone undetected, or at least undramatized and unrestricted. Only Ruth Fuller, of all the adults, had questioned the possibility, and Ramon had denied it successfully.

Maria stopped suddenly in midmovement, like a wave caught cresting in a photograph, contracting her thighs until they met and welded, forcing him out of her. "Ramon," she said with great seriousness, "would you still love me even if we did not do this together?"

He was already wise in the ways of women, prepared for almost any eventuality in the midst of seduction. "You said this was love. If I'm gonna love you, we got to do it, Maria. It is love we're doing."

She moved her slender hands over his ribs, fluting them outward until she could tunnel through his armpits and reach his shoulders from behind. "Love me," she said, her legs blossoming again, the sweet nectar of her ready once more to be extracted, the pistil eager to be pollinated.

He did not like to think of love because he did not really understand it. And so he thought of Ruth Fuller and the day she had brought him a picture book of two naked people embracing in dozens of different positions, and of their attempts to duplicate all of them. He recalled only ten or eleven of them when the memory drew the strings of his sack taut against the base of his cock, forcing him to erupt without warning to Maria.

She looped her arms about his neck at the sudden hot rain drumming the entrance to her. "Love me?" she demanded.

"Yes," he said.

At his affirmation, the rain flooded all of her. She fell back, adrift, and let it sweep her away.

Whether by coincidence or design, on the same morning without school or supervision an unfamiliar car pulled into the short driveway. A familiar woman emerged from it with a strange man.

"Get your robe on, Maria. It's Miss Fuller—Ruth." Ramon inserted himself into a pair of jeans hastily and drew on a shirt.

"Marialita," Ruth Fuller said warmly as the door opened. "And Ramon, of course. This is Mr. Tarradash of the Los Angeles County Department of Adoptions."

"Hello, Maria." He smiled and extended his hand to Ramon. "Hello, Ray."

"Clare and Urban are at the office, am I right?" Ruth asked. She knew the answer and so did not listen for it. "The children call them by their first names," she explained to Tarradash, as though strengthening an indictment.

"Mommy had to go in today," Maria said.

Tarradash glanced at Ruth. "How long have you lived here, Maria?" he asked.

"I don't know. Maybe about six months or a year."

"I think it was closer to four months," Ruth said. "Don't you remember you were at the lake with us this summer, Maria?"

"It doesn't really matter," Tarradash interrupted. "Tell me, children, do you come from Los Angeles originally? In other words, were you born here?"

"San Diego," Maria said.

"No," Ramon contradicted.

"We were there."

"On a visit. But we lived in La Mesa."

"It's not really important," Tarradash said.

"Would you show us your rooms?" Ruth asked.

Maria balked. "Mine is messy. I didn't make my bed yet."

"That's all right, Maria. We don't mind."

Tarradash hesitated. "I think it's a bit irregular, Miss Fuller. We don't exactly have a search warrant."

"Of course, it's all right. They're inviting us to see their rooms, aren't you, Ramon and Maria? Just like you did at Lake St. Clair."

They nodded, confused by the debate over such a simple request. "Mr. Tarradash just wants to make sure you're happy here," Ruth explained. "You are, aren't you?"

There was another unison nod. Both sets of eyes

fixed on the tall, gaunt figure of Tarradash, balding and bespectacled and somehow ominous to them. "The weather is always warm here, isn't it?" he said, trying to be friendly.

"Sometimes at night it gets cold," Ramon said. "It was much warmer in La Mesa."

"Yes, yes. Of course. That's almost Mexico," he agreed.

Maria led them upstairs, pausing at the entrance to her room. A look of mild apprehension moved tangentially over her face and through her eyes. Were adults able to read the settings of sex? The sheets appeared to her to be arranged in a whirl, the pool of still damp juices bull's-eyed in the middle of the target.

She watched Ruth Fuller's eyes carom about the room, ovaling, rounding, squaring, slotting—propelled by some inner curiosity, perhaps some inner knowledge. Yet they seemed to skate over the small lake evaporating in the bed, perhaps unable to accept so obvious a clue, more likely dismissing it as the normal leakage of a high-strung young maiden. One did not make inquiries about liquids upon a bed at any rate.

"Seems like a nice little room. Very adequate," Tarradash said.

"Mine is over here," Ramon said. He led them willingly inside. He had learned to square his corners, military style, in a welfare boys' camp years before and he was proud of his ability.

"Were you ever at Hillside?" Tarradash asked.

"Yes, sir." He beamed at the recognition.

"Congratulations. You still do your bunk Hillside A-Okay." He did not bother to explain that he had begun his social work career as a collegian counselor at Hillside Haven for Boys.

"You should teach your sister how to do that," Ruth Fuller said. She had difficulty keeping her eyes from becoming magnetized by him. The flat nipples of his chest shown darkly through his T-shirt like mementos of summer.

"I will," he said.

"Do you suppose we could see your parents' room since we've seen the others?" Tarradash asked.

"It's downstairs."

They trooped down single file behind Maria.

"Do you ever sleep here?" Ruth Fuller asked, her eyes on Ramon.

"No," Ramon said.

"Not even when you're, say, frightened? Or lonely? Or feeling funny?"

"No," the boy said again.

"Ramon?" she coaxed.

He looked squarely at her. "No," he repeated.

Tarradash had begun the animations of impatience, playing with his fingers at the door. "I think it's time we got going, Miss Fuller. Thank you very much, Ramon, my Hillside boy. And you, too, Maria."

Ruth began to follow him, then hesitated, then turned and brushed Maria's forehead with her lips. Her move toward Ramon was intercepted, his arm moving forward like a rocker, forcing a handshake. She sought his eyes now and he refused them. "Good-bye, Ramon. I hope I'll be seeing you soon again."

"Bye," he said, peering at the floor.

The car had barely cleared the driveway and gotten positioned on the descending road when Clarice Giles swung upward toward the house, too concerned with navigating the steep climb to take note of the passenger in the car passing next to her.

Avery was furious when he learned of the visit. "It's illegal, it's immoral," and there he halted his paraphrasing of Alexander Woollcott. "I'll file charges if you want. . . ."

Legalities made Urban Giles uneasy. He had never lived in a glass house. But too much investigation could turn his home transparent. He chose not to throw the stone Avery offered. "She'll go away," he said. "She's got nothing to go on."

Avery's eyes elevated and crossed him, first horizontally, then vertically. "All right. It's your home and your children."

"Maybe I should talk to her. Find out what she's up to." He had forgotten the terror of their last meeting or he would not even have considered such a step.

"I'm not your attorney, Urban. Quite frankly, we're not even close friends. But I do know you and I am involved in business with you. That entitles me to some sort of participating interest in what the hell happens to you. I say don't talk to her at all. Refuse to meet her under any circumstances——"

"She can be a bitch."

"All women can."

This was his first visit to Avery's home. In his concern over the invasion of Ruth Fuller, he had not given the house its due in attention. It was spectacular, clinging like a white leopard to the face of a canyon, clawing elegantly into the steep profile of western Los Angeles. Despite the dry, almost desert environment, it abounded in carefully nurtured greens, a splashing waterfall and a trio of illuminated pools populated with graceful gold and white fish. At night, from the terrace adjoining the living room, the city became a swarm of lights, a sequined carpet stretching as far as the eye could see. It was an unbelievable dwelling, seeming to resist gravity, gaining a special beauty from the sheer daring of its setting; a stunning body of wood and stone climbing the city's cliffs with animal grace. He could only have meant it to appeal to men. And to devastate women.

"Your place is beyond words, Keith. It's like a Cinerama production." He changed the subject deliberately, fearful of where the original one might lead.

"As a matter of fact, it's been in several movies." He drifted casually over to Urban, who was surveying the dramatic views from the windows, toting the brandy bottle with him. He poured another inch or so into Urban's snifter. "Some screenwriter told me it looked like God built the place for his gardener so he could watch his stars grow. Not too bad for a hack writer, was it?"

"It's just beautiful," Urban said, without commenting on the quote.

They stood in silence for a time, side by side, lost in separate thoughts. It was easier now to proceed slowly, now that he had seen the man in his native habitat.

"That Fuller woman is dangerous," Avery said finally, resuming again. "I'd instruct the children not to talk to her again."

"That's not a simple matter, Keith. While she's here, I'm sure she'll try to contact them again. And they're rather fond of her from last summer. It's not easy to explain these adult complexities to children."

Avery tilted his snifter, holding it to his lips long after he had drained the remaining brandy. Finally, he lowered it, keeping his eyes lost in the swarm of stars beyond the window.

"I want to take Maria to Acapulco with me," he said. "It's a good time for her to be away."

"Where did you get her, Keith? She's absolutely enchanting." Merle Burgess handed out compliments to other females as though each one was forever removed from her own quota, part of herself now the possession of another, a leaf plucked from a tree, a petal from a rose. It was flattery of the highest order.

"Never mind, Merle. I have first option on her if she's for sale. Right, Keith?" Kirk Kimberley interjected.

Avery lay chameleonlike between them, his flat body almost the color of the mahogany deck, his eyes lidded against the crisping sun. Maria had been alternately swimming and sunning herself about the pool near them, her lithe figure bending and curving and straightening, moving from water to deck and back again with fluid grace, engraving an indelible impression in beautiful penmanship upon all who saw her. Her guardian—as he had introduced himself to his hosts—had already decided it was instinctive. He simply could not attribute any of it to the influence of Urban and Clarice Giles. They might occasionally attain a cheap veneer of gentility, but it was never sustained the way Maria had maintained her deportment since their arrival. "She is a little beauty, isn't she? It's hard to believe any parents would abandon a child like that." He moved only his lips, a trace of Emmett Kelly about them due to the white sun-screen cream.

"I assume from what you've said that she's no longer available," Kirk Kimberley continued despite the presence of Merle. She was the only woman in his current life who had no reason to be after his income, rumored to be in six figures daily and pick-your-own-multiple annually. Merle Burgess might not approach these totals, but her wealth was spread over three continents with villas and ranches and estates, all maintained out of her daddy's legacies, not dependent upon the whims of anyone but herself. And she was, despite the strain of a half century of *la dolce vita,* still beautiful. It was Kimberley who sought her company, not vice versa, despite all the gossip to the contrary.

"Everyone alive is available, Kirk, dear, in one sense or another. Precisely what did you have in mind? I mean besides *that?"* Keith could not see the evolution of her look from savage to primitive to coyly sophisticated. He would have appreciated its range. But he did scramble to his feet at this exchange of volleys over him. They were both too valuable to him, even for name-dropping, to risk any misunderstanding involving him.

"I think, Merle, that Kirk was thinking in terms of adoption or foster-home arrangements. We've talked about it from time to time."

She threw her head back and laughed lustily, her long neck swanning. "Keith, dear, you are such an outrageous liar. I'm sure that's why you're such a successful lawyer."

He laughed politely. "I really think Kirk would

make an excellent father for Maria," he said with a careful mixture of seriousness and lightness. "Unfortunately, though, our little girl's off the adoption market. I just rescued her from her new parents for a few days. It's a moral obligation as the legal intermediary in the proceedings to keep an eye on her during the first year. I don't really have to do it——"

"My, wouldn't it be just a little more interesting if there was just a teeny-weeny little bit of an immoral obligation involved, too? Don't you think so, Kirk?"

The multimillionaire watched the yacht's tender approaching, slicing through the froth of Acapulco Bay, deliberately keeping his eyes off the girl while Merle was watching him. "Remember that couple we met in Beirut last year, dear? One of them was from London— the man, I think it was—and the woman was either from Brussels or Brittany, I forget which. At any rate, it doesn't matter. Keith, you wouldn't believe it, but they were both well into their fifties, I'd say, rather successful in the import-export business, but not really overly affluent, which is irrelevant. But, at any rate, to give you the proper picture, they were also rather pedestrian looking, quite unattractive in fact by Acapulco standards, and they lived in this huge old Moorish castle, which was also their office and warehouse. I'm digressing again, but we had gone there on the recommendation of a Parisian dealer in antiquities whom Merle has patronized for years, looking for some rare Egyptian metallics she wanted for her place in Majorca. The references must have been excessive, at least mine, because the couple insisted we stay and join them for dinner.

"Well, Keith, here's the point I was getting at—there

were four of the most stunning children you ever did see, all about your girl's age, walking about the place, cavorting merrily, friendly and all that despite the fact we didn't speak their language, and they were all stark naked. Two girls and two boys, obviously not their own—not merely because of their considerably better looks, mind you, but their much darker skin tone, kind of a milk-chocolate, I'd say. To make conversation, because neither of our hosts seemed inclined to offer either introductions or explanations, I finally said something like 'My, what attractive children.' And then the woman, Madame Pleshette, if I recall correctly, spoke up and said, 'Yes, that's why we bought them.'

"Well, at first I was sure I'd misunderstood or else she was making some sort of Lebanese joke, but we soon found out they really had purchased them from a dealer in live flesh right there in the city, not for parental purposes at all, but for their own pleasure whenever they felt like it. In fact, they offered us our choice of the four if we wanted to stay for the night. Now, isn't that something, going on right now in a civilized society in the latter part of the twentieth century?"

Merle Burgess had lowered herself onto a chaise longue during Kimberley's lengthy meandering, her eyes hooded with large sunglasses which hid boredom or enthusiasm with equal effectiveness. "Kirk hasn't been the same since," she said flatly. "I was afraid he might go out and buy the whole female population for himself."

"It's a fascinating story, Kirk," Avery said, as though he had never heard it before. It was to him the single most annoying attribute of the superrich, this tendency toward repetition, as though their lives had been dulled by an excess of dazzle, just as lesser lives were blunted by routine and hopelessness. Merle Burgess had also made the same comment at the end of Kimberley's recitation before. Was it possible that neither of them even vaguely realized that having heard a similar version of the same story several times before, he had gradually, cautiously, but deliberately, revealed ever more intimate details of his own activities to them, ingratiating himself via these very intimacies, culminating for the present with his selection of Maria to be the first of his protégés to be presented in their royal court of wealth and prestige?

He signaled Maria to join them only moments before the tender drew alongside the yacht, filled to capacity with the daily aquatic parade of celebrities and socialites, all shedding the jaded looks they normally wore ashore, suddenly animated and fawning, witty and debonair, as they rose into the range of vision of the reigning monarch of their society and his chosen queen.

Avery found sham transluscent, clear enough to make him wary, but sufficiently diffuse to keep him intrigued. "Kirk," he whispered as Merle took her welcoming position near the boarding ladder, "I want to take Maria down to "The Ghetto" for hamburgers and rock music. Why don't you come with us?"

The multimillionaire was multi-intrigued. "You know, I've never been down there."

"All the more reason to come. Just for a little change. You see most of these people all season."

"Please?" Maria said beguilingly, clasping his arm.

"Dammit, I think I will. Nobody'll even notice I'm not around."

"That's the boy, Kirk. I'll tell the captain. Then he can tell Merle later if she gets worried. Or curious."

Kimberley went through the ritual of greeting each of his guests individually, being introduced to those few he was meeting for the first time according to the rules of protocol. When his task was completed, he scrambled agilely over the rail, down the rope-and-wood ladder into the spacious stern of the tender, catching Maria with generous hands, bolstering her bosom as she pitched gaily into his arms. Keith speeded their departure by bringing the end of the main line aboard with him. It was the first time he had ever tried to separate Kirk Kimberley from Merle Burgess. In reality, it was the first time he had ever dared. It was a gamble and he wondered now at what odds he was playing.

"The Ghetto" was not a generic term for the area. It had been coined by Keith on a previous visit and gained some measure of acceptance in the Kimberley crowd because it captured the essence of their attitude toward the influx of bargain jetters camping in once-fashionable hotels along the *costa,* and the Coney Island cluster of pizza parlors, hamburger stands and snack shops which had festered there catering to the newcomers. People like Kimberley and Merle Burgess retained a degree of aloofness from the riffraff by remaining anchored in Acapulco Bay, where the illusion of the resort's past elegance and exclusivity was enhanced by distance. But even there the new pollution touched them with islands of scum clouding the bay's surface like huge, floating lily pads. The sight of them had kept her confined by choice to the yacht for more than a month. It was not surprising that the gregarious Kimberley welcomed the chance to mingle with a less pretentious element for a change, especially with two such stimulating companions as Keith Avery and Maria Giles.

He was buoyant and effusive on the ferry trip over, lamenting the water pollution but taking a much more democratic attitude toward the beach-and-hotel variety. "These charters are good," he told his guests. "It gives more people a chance to enjoy this lovely place and this beautiful climate."

"Wait until you see the girls, Kirk. They may be poor economically, but their bodies look like goldmines."

He touched the brim of his yachting cap, watching the enlarging shoreline. "I'm sure there isn't one of them any prettier than our Maria," he said.

She smiled upward into his tanned, angular face, her teeth white as Egyptian lotus against her own lightly auburn face. She had hurriedly pulled on a snowy twill yachting outfit Keith had bought for her in a hotel shop the day before. Her bikini beneath it was still damp against her flesh. She was very much a woman physically, an exceptionally lovely woman, whatever the distance between body and emotional maturity. It did not matter to either of them anyway. They rather enjoyed their imagined edge over her, just as they were enchanted by her youthful vivacity and the lingering illusion of innocence.

"Where are you staying, anyway, Keith?"

"Villa Vera. Right in the heart of The Ghetto." He

laughed at his own suggestion that so luxurious a hotel could ever be so classified, whatever the change in its clinetele.

"Good. At least we'll have a place to run to if there's a Ghetto uprising." He grinned at what he intended as a joke. "Incidentally, Keith, you're welcome to stay with us, of course. Forgive me for not suggesting that to both of you earlier. It completely slipped my mind."

"Thanks, Kirk. But it's Maria's first visit and having a land base gives us a lot more flexibility in getting around."

"I understand. But remember, you're always welcome aboard the *Andromeda*."

Keith Avery never moved without interior calculation. He knew, of course, that he could have contacted Kimberley in advance and been invited to make the yacht his home and headquarters. He had done just that a number of times in past seasons. But he wanted very much to introduce Maria to Acapulco in his own fashion first, without the distractions of a multimillionaire and a floating paradise. Now that they were acquainted intimately, now that he could read more intelligently the special biological formula of her, he was ready, even eager, to pursue once more his basic hobby of collecting and maintaining a stable of rich and beautiful and influential friends. Any man with half a face and physique could simply collect women. That put a very pedestrian limitation on both his imagination and his potential, as Keith Avery saw it.

"Can we go dancing?" Maria said. Her eyes were incandescent even against the fiery sunset.

"That sounds like great fun," Kirk said.

Avery played every situation, every conversation, as

though life was a continuing match of wits with point totals to be added up at its conclusion. The looseness and the nonchalance he affected were carefully programmed from within. He seldom lost control of either himself or those he was manipulating.

"Telepathy," he said. "I already have a table for us at Perdido."

"Goody."

Kimberley caught fire with her, kindled by her youth against the flint of his age. "You've got to come into the organization, Keith. You're a genius at everything."

They followed the *costa,* picking their way through the loops and knots and strands of tourists, past the Pizza Hut, Kelly's Hamburgers, Sam's Roast Beef Sandwich, the Big Boy Snack Shop, a Tastee Freeze, into a brief stretch of the old, refined Acapulco which had originally attracted men of Kimberley's stature and transformed the resort into an international playground for the wealthy. Most of what remained had tarnished, but there were still the yachts in the bay and stunning new homes rising among the elegant old estates— enough jewels to make the proliferating zircons tolerable to the people who attended Kimberley's daily parties aboard the *Andromeda.*

"Where is Keith?" Maria asked. They had been walking for almost half an hour and she had lost sight of him.

"On the beach," Kirk said. He watched as she fielded admiring glances from strutting males peacocking along her path. He did not blame them. His own eyes had difficulty breaking away.

"Come on down here," Keith called to them.

"Let's walk along the beach, too," she said to Kirk.

"Look at this sign," Keith greeted them. "If my high school Spanish serves me properly it reads, 'This is a Place for Families. We ask Adequate Norms of Comportment and Conduct."

"Pretty good. But it probably says, 'No bikinis on women over two hundred and fifty pounds.'"

"Hey, we've got a comedian with us, Maria." He was surprised by Kimberley's abandon and light spirits. He had never seen him quite so loose before.

The *Andromeda* was distant but visible from where they stood. "Merle hasn't sent up any flares yet," Kirk said.

"Let's go dancing now," Maria said.

"I think the lady has a point," he agreed.

"We're off," Keith said.

What Perdido lacked in motif, it more than made up for in kinetic energy. A five-piece band of long-haired Mexican youths segued from one hard-rock number into another without a break.

"Come on, Kirk," Maria urged.

He got up with some apprehension, but much determination. When he reached out for her, she wiggled away. "No, no," she said. "I will come to you later." With such a promise, he endured the desperations of the floor and shook himself as violently as everyone else about him was doing.

"Wow, Kirk, you are wild!" she called out as his body snaked and shuddered. By the end of the dance, he was fighting for breath. Keith took over and did his thing through another prolonged marathon, returning finally to recruit Kirk again. In an hour of alternating roles, with Maria on the floor throughout, the two men exhausted themselves. Their clothes were as wet as if they had jumped into the bay.

"I think we should all go up to the room and take a shower," Keith suggested. They had finally wound her down enough to gain agreement.

"Maybe we can come back later," she said as they left.

"Maybe."

In the room, it was almost too simple because it was so natural. Maria merely stepped out of her clothes and they did the same. It was a meeting of the minds and they had met somewhere during the past hour at Perdido with the sweet musk of her body to perfume the communion.

Keith took a secondary role in deference to Kirk. After all, he had already explored her repeatedly and could endure a brief wait for another opportunity.

She was aroused from the heat of her body and the sensual dancing and she went to him without hesitation, placing herself before him to enter as he wished. Only the sound of breathing traveled the room until his face brought his lips audibly against the seething middle of her, into the wild jungle of her crotch. He slipped his nose over the velvety layers, beavering through the mossy dampness, leading his eager tongue into coral flutters, rippling the secret flesh of her, hidden from view like some forbidden blossom. His tongue probed the petals with starved dedication, sucking in the sweet nectar in unashamed slurpings, sensing it enter him, traveling through him to await escape in the crowded terminal of his cock.

It was not enough for Keith to confine himself to mere circling of them as the involvement deepened. He had gorged himself on her since their arrival and yet his appetite was insatiable. She writhed under the relentless tonguing of Kimberley and he stood fondling the fierce hard-on the scene induced, finally unable to restrain himself any longer. He waved his long cock about her face until her eyes opened, and then her mouth, and then the meeting, awkward at first until he could organize himself with them, kneeling over her face, his balls rolling about her chin, tightening to the pull of her tongue. He watched it all upside down, peering between his outstretched arms to see her suck him frantically; looking beyond, down the length of her flawless torso, meeting the haunted eyes of Kimberley over the horizon of her cunt, his head bobbing wildly against it. He squeezed his eyes shut as the cheeks of his ass tightened, seeming to pull all of his organs into one terrible knot. And then the sweet pain, almost unbearable until it spurted from him in joyous globs, breaking against her lips and face, running down the lovely profile, nesting in the ribbons of black satin hair about her neck.

She had all but strangled Kirk as she met climax with climax, wrapping her legs about his head, forcing him deeper into her, enveloping his entire face with the pink leaves gathered at the meeting of her limbs, pumping the sump buried deeper behind them, the suction making rich liquid sounds between them. Then, suddenly, she rose, her face still gleaming with the residue of love, and drove Kimberley onto his back, sprawling from the surprise assault, his cock an acute angle to his body. With athletic grace, with almost engineering precision, she slid herself onto him, rising and falling in the new position, up and down, varying her tempo instinctively, the inner folds of her vagina like a puppet clam subject to her direction, clutching and freeing, freeing and clutching the tender tip of him until everything he was, everything he wanted to be, was gathered there. She responded to him with the soft curves of her body, kissing his lidded eyes with parted mouth, her hot breath syncopated to the rhythm of her cheeks. Her cunt grew taut and she slid it along the full length of him, skinning it without releasing it until the friction set it aflame. Then it burst, a fountain of white lava shooting uncontrolled into her, against the ripe, haired lips, leaping the horizon of her thighs, splashing up to her navel, gloriously full, emptying him, cleansing him, purging him.

Keith walked him back to the pier. The tender was waiting and they said little except good-bye. Tomorrow was another day.

Life had a way, especially when things were sunnyside up, of reaching in and scrambling the contents. Avery had planned on three days, extended them to five, then reached for two more and discovered he had not only thinned his personal strength but his professional self as well.

"Some state senator's started an investigation of Pacific Place," his private secretary reported by phone. "They've already questioned Urban Giles."

There was no outward alarm in his reaction. Coolness under fire was a professional requisite for men who traded in child futures, who daily wove themselves in and around laws created by jurists who were either unwilling or unable to gauge the ability of others to circumvent them. Children were sacrosanct to law-makers, even children whose physical attributes qualified them for early recognition as adults. They had mass support, of course. That made acceptance all the more delusory as far as he was concerned, all the easier to stretch and bend and violate.

Keith Avery, in all his eloquent dapperness, in his outspoken concern for the welfare of his wards, was above ordinary suspicion. Like so many of his Holly-wood friends, he was an actor. The difference was that he gave daily Academy Award performances, without a script, without a rehearsal, without a contract.

Merle Burgess was mad about the night. "Men are all the same, all sons-of-bitches," she told Keith on the eve of their departure. "They want the whole works—experience, tenderness, understanding, love—all tossed into pretty little disposable packages."

"Merle, dear," he said, "you're the one woman of all the women I've known who must look at the desper-ations of other females and feel comfortable. There's no substitute for classic beauty, no way to get it if you haven't got it. You're one of the blessed and I hope you appreciate it." In all his career he had never felt so close to certifying a relationship as he did currently with Kirk Kimberley. He wanted her to continue to like him and he succeeded.

"You're full of it, Keith. But thanks for wasting some of your eloquence on me."

They left hurriedly, man and child, Keith scooping Maria from the rope ladder dangling over the side of the *Andromeda,* looking upward into the pained face of Kirk Kimberley. For all his millions, he was not free. "Good-bye, Maria," He dropped the farewell over the side with a sense of finality, unwanted but inevitable.

"Good-bye, Kirk. Good-bye, Merle." Her voice sang out over the mutter of the tender's engine.

"I'll call you from L.A.," Keith promised.

The tender pulled away with an abrupt roar and no more messages could be flung over the water.

"I like it here," Maria said as they boarded the plane.

"You'll be back," he said.

The morning after intruded obesely, fat with sun and pregnant with problems. He had kept Maria with him overnight, half anticipating a final fling, but a series of phone calls robbed him of both time and incentive.

Urban was at Keith's offices to reclaim his treasure. It was strange, this transference of a child between two men who knew her intimately, yet played such disparate roles in her life.

"You got sun, Maria."

"Not too much. I was inside a lot."

"She looks great, Keith."

"She always looks great."

"How's Ramon?" Maria asked.

"You'll see him in a little while. Now wait for me, please, outside."

"What's the story on the state thing?" Avery asked as soon as the door closed behind her.

"They're on to it," he replied gravely.

"On to what, Urb? There's nothing to get on to." His voice was reedy with annoyance. "We're registered, we're certified, we pay our taxes. And we run a legit fund-raising operation for a humane public-service venture. What the hell's to investigate?"

"They forced me to accompany them to Pacific Place."

"So what happened?"

"You should be okay. But they're getting a file on me."

Avery looked willow slim behind the sharp creases of his suit, a thin smile paralleling his shoulders, a short horizontal line drawn against the straight vertical of his body. It was a noticeable contrast to the slouched figure of Urban Giles, broadening at the hips, a small rise of belly detracting from an otherwise flat profile.

"Something you forgot to tell me?"

"Not really."

"I guess I don't have to know it now, then."

"No."

"Okay. Let it all ride till the train crashes."

He got up and moved slowly to the door, pausing as if to say something, then continuing without a word. "Let's go home, Maria," he said.

Chapter Seventeen

Avery was cornered.

His suavity had lacquered much of his life, but he could not paint over the flaws indefinitely. The whole structure of his operation was weak, the veneer thin. It could hold up among the superficial people who populated his business and social life, but it could not withstand serious investigation. He was a bona fide member of the film-world social set, which implied living and entertaining lavishly, but there were no requirements for admission beyond these. No one really knew much about him. No one really cared. He was as valid as his credit with his caterer, as important as his latest mention in the *Los Angeles Times*.

Urban Giles had not even entered the outermost periphery of the Avery set. By caste standards, he was an untouchable, a mere servant. The proof of it, in a minor way, was his continuing difficulty with the Beverly Hills police. Every time he chose to wander through the community, he was subjected to the interrogation they gave vagrant strangers. This despite his own conception of himself as a man of distinction. It rankled and humiliated him, but he was in no position to alert any police anywhere of his total identity. And so he suffered it, along with his other emotional malignancies.

Avery frayed under the stress. He became understandably impatient and irritable as stories began quilting the pages of the papers, patchy at first but with steadily longer and more detailed colorings as the days progressed. The boiler room was in limbo for the time, too hot to continue operating. Yet he kept Urban reporting there as a sort of custodian of the machinery, certain that his legal adroitness would have everything repaired imminently. But as doubt mounted, it became his target for releasing the mounting frustration which accompanied it. For some inexplicable reason, he seemed to hold Giles responsible for the dilemma in which he had mired himself.

"You've been running a real two-bit, amateur operation here," he accused him. "That Fuller woman left something out of her rundown on you: incompetent."

Urban was in no benevolent mood himself with another dent in the tin life he tried to pretend was silver. But he kept his blood at 212° Fahrenheit, bubbling slightly but not at a rolling boil, by the addition of the chemicals gin and vermouth. There seemed no useful purpose in responding to Avery's provocations—until he appeared unannounced and unexpected at their home one night.

"Where's Maria?" he demanded in the chill voice which marked a hostile state of drunkenness in him.

"It's late, Keith. She's already asleep."

"Wake her up, then. I want her to sleep with me tonight."

"For God's sake, Keith. I can't let you do a thing like that."

"I'll get her myself then." He lurched toward the stairs and Urban moved swiftly to block his path.

"There are some rules, Keith, even to the lowest game."

Keith's eyes flared, the suppressed sense of superiority rising from submersion along with his hostility. "Out of my way, old-timer," he snarled. "You could be doing twenty years——"

Diminished he was, but not down for the count. "My twenty against yours," he said defiantly.

Avery rammed him, full-shouldered. "I said I want to fuck her," he enunciated, biting off each word as he swept past the startled body. But his foot had barely touched the first step when Urban recovered, snaking himself forward until he was able to dig his nails into the ascending ankle. "Son-of-a-bitch!" Avery screamed as he folded to his knees.

"Daddy!" Maria shouted from the top of the stairs. She did not immediately recognize Keith Avery. By the time she did, they were a tangle of bodies locked in contorted holds from which neither could escape without the consent of the other. Avery's attache case had flown from his hands, striking the floor and breaking open, its contents spilling for a radius of several yards. It gave the impression they had been arguing over business, an impression which was erased even for Maria by Urban's seething warning. "I'll kill you if you ever come near her again," he said through vised teeth.

Finally, sensing a limpness in his opponent's ligaments, Urban turned his grip fluid and slowly rose to his feet. Avery got up and brushed himself rapidly with the palms of his hands. With the thrashing movements of a harvesting machine, he gathered up his papers, stuffed them into his case and swung the door open.

"I'll be back for you, Maria," he said coolly now. "As for you, Giles, you're through." With that, he thrust himself through the doorway, slamming the door behind him.

Urban permitted him to reach the driveway before delivering an epitaph. "If I'm through, Avery," he announced with an evenness of delivery belying his own turmoil, "then you're through, too."

It was considerably more than an idle threat.

A house of cards, one reporter called it. The simile was not altogether valid, but the collapse of the fund, of Pacific Place and a series of adoption agencies followed in such rapid sequence that it was a quite natural figure of speech to employ. Keith Avery was octopean in the numbers and angles of his far-reaching operations in the business of acquiring and merchandising children. Despite the penetrating revelations, however, he was surprisingly unshakable in the publicity spotlight, almost as though he had been preparing all his life to occupy center stage and discuss himself. Not unexpectedly, a flood of California women, ever receptive to new tangents of celebrity and glamour, began to lionize the dapper attorney with the fabled life-style and the Lolita appetite. He was a natural for the tabloids and the fan magazines. As might be anticipated, they rushed to enshrine him.

Urban and Clarice withdrew behind the blinds and drapes and shades of their house, as they had done elsewhere before, resuming the furtiveness which had never totally left them since their exodus to California. They were inevitably linked to the Avery enterprises, and just as inevitably the press file on their past was uncovered and reactivated in terms of a whole new episode in their episodic lives. But none of it penetrated the carefully smoothed outward calm of Urban until the weekly *Los Angeles Tartarus* appeared on the stands with a front-page feature titled "A Week of Wanton Wickedness in Acapulco." Liberally illustrated, it listed a cast headed by Kirk Kimberley, Keith Avery and Maria Giles, with supporting roles assigned to Merle Burgess and the captain of the *Andromeda*. It was clearly a production of the Mexican *paparrazzi*—telephoto lenses, blurred shots implying all sorts of assignations and deviations, sharply accented adult-vs.-child photographs, and dangerous implications regarding the foster parentage of the young beauty under siege. He was instantaneously alarmed.

"I hate to do this to you again, Clare," he said that night, "but we've got to get out of here. The authorities will probably follow up on this, and Jasper's sure to get wind of it. Plus we've got the Toledo crowd still looking for revenge."

"What do we tell the children this time? That we're gypsies, Urban?" Her voice was worn, an old needle rutting along an even older record. It was hard to imagine her so recently playing the game of youth.

"I think it's best if we don't tell them. We'll make it an adventure instead."

She smiled ruefully. "What about the state? The investigators?"

"There are no charges filed against me. Not yet. I'm

not ducking anything by leaving. If we hesitate, though, that old saying could come true. We could be lost."

Her sigh came from deep in the well of her emotions. "All right," she said. "I'll start packing."

He diluted the immediate pain with his favorite remedy, letting its warmth wash over the cold realities. Hours later, hearing her rummaging about the closets, he moved heavily into their bedroom and watched in silence as she folded sheets and pillowcases, here and there interspersed with some small prize of the past, a doily reading "God Bless Our Home" which her mother had embroidered half a century before, an album of pictures from their wedding day, a set of silver candlesticks which she never found occasion to use anymore.

"Good thing we never did have that party," he said finally, cutting into the silence.

"What party is that, Urb?" she asked patiently.

"Those kids from Maria's class. And Ramon's. You know the one I was planning."

She felt as though she were curling all of a sudden, her shoulders and neck bowing over like a tree weighted late in the season and unharvested. "It is a good thing, Urb," she said quietly.

He was smiling, liquid all over his teeth and lips. "Finally thought of one smart thing I did lately." He patted her rump with something akin to affection. She could not tell for sure—she had forgotten the difference. "You're a good gal, Clare," he said. "How about a little celebration drink?"

It was so ludicrous, she was forced to laugh. "Celebrate? I might have one for the wake, if that's what you mean."

Drinking company is what he sought. The premise was really quite secondary. He displayed surprising agility, considering his consumption, in fetching the bottle and an extra glass for her. "To the celebration and the wake," he said when her glass had been filled and delivered to her. "Another chapter in the continuing life saga of Clarice and Urban Giles."

"We'll survive," she said after the Scotch had varnished her throat and stomach.

"Survive? Clare, *surmount* is the word. I've been thinking about doing another telethon somewhere out here. Maybe Phoenix or Tucson or one of those boomtowns."

"You're forgetting the unions, Urb. They never forget and never forgive."

"I've thought about that, too. We've got a few bucks. All I have to do is get a couple local business agents in my corner. It won't cost a helluva lot, Clare."

She returned to folding clothing, inserting each newly condensed garment into one of the three cases lying like open books on the floor. "You should get some sleep. If we're leaving tomorrow, it'll be a big day."

"I feel good," he said. He had psyched himself up and was feeling confident again. It mattered little to him at the moment that he was abandoning a sinking ship with no other real vessel on the horizon. After a while, buoyed by his new rationale, he rose and moved unsteadily toward the hall.

"Going to bed?" she asked.

"I'm gonna peek into Maria's room," he said, a little

curl of laughter trailing his words. "Does that answer your question?"

Clarice lost herself in the sheets she was now folding. Living with him never got any easier.

He was a fugitive again and yet he was unable to accept or admit that the sudden exodus of the Giles family was an escape and not an impromptu variation in an adventurous life. This romanticizing of himself and his activities had been a lifelong self-deception. Clarice accepted it with resignation, more concerned over its effect on the children than upon herself and her husband.

A plan, more accurately a scheme, had formulated in Urban's mind during his long night's impotency. He deluded himself sexually as he did vocationally, refusing to recognize the limitations imposed by age and alcohol. In tandem, they were a destructive combination. But he had fumbled about for hours, convinced of his own virility and desirability, robbing the girl of much-needed sleep while he struggled vainly to force an erection. Eventually he had given up, blaming the mental pressure of departure for his failure to perform. It was during the predawn interlude that followed, sitting alone in the kitchen sipping whiskey straight from the bottle to insure silence, that he had hit upon a Gilesian inspiration.

They would go to Acapulco.

Clarice heard him shuffling about in his new excitement, unaware he had solved a personal dilemma but acutely aware of the last solution preceding their departure from Elmhill. These thoughts, so long submerged, rose to wrestle her mind as she tried to sleep.

"What's the matter, Urb? What are you doing dancing around the kitchen at this hour?" She had drifted in and out of a nightmarish kind of slumber, haunted with multiple anxieties, hearing the muffled voices emerging from Maria's room, wondering all the while what lay in store for all of them, fearful his old paranoia would return and expand and destroy all of them.

"Sit down, sit down," he insisted, humming snatches of "The World Is Waiting for the Sunrise" as he skated about, waving a boxful of stick matches for no apparent reason.

"What are the matches for?" she asked, fully awake at that instant.

He looked at his hand, unmistakably surprised by its contents. "Damn," he said. "I was going to light the stove, I guess. Yeah, that's it. To make some coffee for breakfast. You like coffee, Clare."

"Put them down, Urb. Please? You know we have an electric percolator."

He did as she requested, looking vague and remote, then almost simultaneously bright and enthusiastic. "I've got it all figured out. Everything. First we're going to Mexico for a few days."

"Urb, this is no time for a vacation."

He frowned with exaggerated effort, giving his face the furrowed effect of a circus clown. "Will you let me do the planning around here? I said we're going to Mexico. I didn't say anything about a vacation. . . ."

He fell asleep over his coffee, a welcome respite for her, enabling her to expedite final packing for their

departure. It was difficult, but she did try not to think
of the newly acquired furnishings they were forced to
abandon. Only she, along with him of course, knew
they would not be returning.

"Can we take our bikes?" Maria asked.

"I'm afraid not," Clarice answered. "They'll have to
wait here till you get back." The Christmas things, for
some odd reason, were among the most difficult for her
to include among the expendables. It had been the
single memorable holiday of recent years and she
would have liked to retain a small token of it. Other
than the Bosom-Buddy.

"One of my bed dolls, please? Just one?" Maria
begged.

"Just one," Clarice agreed.

En route that day, somewhere near La Mesa where
the children were born, they stopped to rest. Urban
found a newsstand near the center of town which carried the Los Angeles papers. He sat in the car and
searched them carefully while Ramon and Maria disappeared into the countryside, ostensibly off on a
nostalgic walk back into the memory of childhood.
Clarice grew concerned over their long absence, but
she stared quietly into the papers with her husband,
not wanting to upset him further on their strained
journey.

She was resigned now to the fact of the children's
lovemaking. Her chief concern was keeping him from
discovering it. Why, she could not even explain fully to
herself. It was perhaps that his ego had been subjected
to so much abuse lately she feared the effect of such a
revelation. As for herself, everything had changed once
more in recent weeks. The advent of Ruth Fuller, the

discovery of Ramon and Maria as more than brother and sister, the collapse of their economic security, had devastated her, all but neutralizing her libido. She now believed again that all she had ever wanted was simply Urban Giles. All the rest of it, she rationalized, she had gone along with primarily to please him.

So she thought. So she believed. It failed to explain why she was jealous of the children now, separately and together. Or why she wished and dreamed repeatedly they were back in New York once more, childless, working together day and night building telethons out of blue sky and wishbones, pledges and promises.

A sense of almost tactile relief gripped both front-seat occupants when the car passed easily over the border near Tijuana. They were now in the land of improbable extradition, at least as far as any of their assorted real and imagined *crimes* were concerned. An air of gaiety, of abandon even, entered and displaced the tenseness as they rolled through Mexicali and swung down the western coastline of Mexico toward their destination. They stopped overnight in Culiacán, the capital of Sinaloa, depending upon the children for translations and interpretations. English was spoken by most of the businessmen catering to tourists, but they themselves took advantage of the linguistic abilities of Ramon and Maria to go native in dining and accommodations.

On the following morning, en route to Acapulco, Urban hit upon another inspiration of Gilesian proportions. They would rent a boat there and live aboard it for several days in celebration of Maria's fifteenth birthday, which fell on the day following. She displayed her burgeoning maturity after the deal was set by graciously making no comparison between the aging cruiser and the sleek white yacht on which she had spent part of her previous visit to the resort. Besides, now Ramon was there to enjoy the climate Kimberley had celebrated and that made a substantial difference. Of course, Maria had no inkling or awareness that her foster father was in any way interested in the *Andromeda* and its illustrious owner.

"Champagne?" Clarice questioned as he clambered aboard with supplies. "For the children?"

"Stop calling them children, for God's sake. Maria'll be fifteen tomorrow. In a few months, Ramon'll be seventeen. They're people, not kids."

She was beyond objecting. The tempo of their recent life left little opportunity for reflection or regret. They were living a *now* existence, with only a present and no past or future. It violated her personal code of security, but she endured it as she had everything before. After only hours in Acapulco, she had even begun, reluctantly, to enjoy the therapeutic combination of sun and water.

The long trip down had been debilitating, particularly the long stretches between libations, as far as Urban was concerned. Because of it, because of all the direct and subtle pressures pushing and pulling him until a few hours before, he postponed immediate action on his plan involving Kirk Kimberley. Most important now was the celebration of little Maria's big birthday.

Whistles, suggestive shouts and unabashed propositions followed her everywhere in the uninhibited Latin resort. It was a relief to all four of them to get the boat away from the pier, out into the relative privacy of the bay. They anchored beyond the larger clusters of ships, selecting a fairly isolated expanse of water which few swimmers could reach and other boatmen seemed to be shunning.

Ramon eased overboard immediately, while Urban opened the first bottle and poured portions for all of them. "Hey, Ramon," Maria shouted gaily, "come back and drink to my birthday!" She passed a glass to him as he bobbed in place alongside the boat, treading water as he sipped.

Champagne, as every experienced drinker knows, has exhilarating and aphrodisiac effects upon certain people, particularly those unfamiliar with its chemistry. Two glasses of the sparkling potion and Maria stripped off her bikini, diving dramatically into the water for a brief frolic in its pleasant warmth. They had all succumbed to the combination of sun and wine, the mood of *sans souci,* after the long descent from Los Angeles. Clarice did not even voice an objection to the nudity. When Maria emerged, the sight of her—moisture clinging like round diamonds to her nipples and the breasts beneath them, her hair polished by the sea until it gleamed brilliantly in the massive sun, tiny pearls of wetness ornamenting the T-shaped shrubbery of her crotch, her cheeks of rich cream huddled behind her, reaching below to barely hide the entrance to her—fermented the champagne to new degrees of potency within Urban Giles.

They sat about the boat's rear cockpit, using the narrow rim of deck as a bench, legs dangling into its open square. It was the first time in her life Maria had been high, far above her natural exuberance, and she laughed and bubbled without reservation to every challenge and suggestion.

"Maria, you have more than one mouth to feed," Urban suggested impishly, pointing to the pink furrows at the apex of her legs. He leaned over, pushing aside the erection which sprang up instantly, and refilled her glass.

"All of me is having a birthday," she agreed, "so all of me should have some champagne."

Ramon was hard now, too, his excitement detailed against the tight cover of his trunks. He was not overly familiar with alcohol, either, having been drunk only once in his life on red wine with a friend at summer camp. It was difficult for him to gauge what it was doing to him now, but he did not care because he felt good and the party was getting interesting.

Maria parted the voiceless lips with sure fingers, placing the rim of her glass between them, tilting it just enough to release a trickle of the tawny liquid into herself. "Ooh," she giggled, "that tickles."

Urban put down his individual bottle after sucking another elongated swallow through its neck, dropping to his knees in front of her. "A kiss for your birthday, little Maria," he said, pressing his own lips against the soft garnet petals before him, suppressing his tongue temporarily out of respect for his tribute and the occasion.

"Ramon," he said, arising, "you're next."

The boy hesitated, his grin half-bashful, half-intoxicated.

"Come on," Urban urged. "Don't tell me you never kissed one of these before?"

He bent down without further prompting, brushing

the springy hair quickly with his lips. "Happy birthday," he said.

Clarice watched the male preening and genuflections silently, controlling the volatile mix of alcohol, jealousy and libido in the caldron of her body. She, too, found inhibitions slipping from her and she made less and less effort to restrain their departure. Abruptly she swung herself into the sunken area and approached Ramon, pulling his cock from under the bathing suit. It loomed larger than ever as it strained against the tight elastic. She fell upon it as though it might escape at any moment.

There was no longer any need for words or preliminaries as all four of them wriggled from the last traces of clothing impeding their bodies, intertwining in a slippery puzzle of arms and legs and tits and cocks and cunts, writhing on the hard deck like worms, the only comfort sought in the soft, wet orifices of one another. Champagne passed among them, through them, lubricating areas untouched by the oils and juices of passion, joining to speed the frictionless flight of time, the golden day alloying with night's silver, an amethyst dusk thrown over everything about them.

It was then that the ferret eyes of Urban Giles detected the change in her. "Mama Clare," he said with a mixture of amusement and surprise, "what happened to you?"

Maria followed his eyes to their target and she, too, experienced a similar reaction. "How did it get like *that?*" she gasped.

With the addition of Ramon, all eyes were now upon the tillage of her crotch, its furrows barren and wrinkled, shorn of their crop of hairy curlicues. "I shaved it," Clarice said. "Like it?" She thrust the apparatus of her vagina forward, leaning backward at the same sime to accentuate the presentation.

"It sure looks raw," Urban said.

"That's the way mine used to be," Maria said.

"I wanted it to be like a little girl's again," Clarice confessed. She fingered the lips of it as though she were modeling it.

"Jesus, Clare, you must be getting senile. You know how long it takes for that to grow back? Pubic hair takes forever."

"I propose we all drink a toast to it," she said, ignoring the negatives. "It's the birthday of the new me. Right, Maria?"

Maria attributed it all to the champagne, which made it all easier to assimilate and accept. Prior to now, she had heard much from her father in the way of promiscuous talk and action, but Clarice had always somehow stayed just outside the sexual arena as far as she was concerned. "It looks big and happy," she said.

Her forefinger traveled over the red whorl, skating through a thin film of moisture her exhibitionism had deposited there. "Say something nice about it, too, Urban," she said.

He was prancing about the small cockpit in a mocking dance, jiggling his balls in one hand, sucking from a bottle of champagne with the other. At her request, he halted before her and pretended to be inspecting her offering. "Looks awfully meaty," he said solemnly. "Must be two pounds in the folds alone."

Maria and Ramon laughed joyously at the inflection of his voice and the facetiousness of his words. "All

right, just for that, Mr. Bigmouth," Clarice said in
feigned anger, "I want you to show everybody that you
love it this way. I want you to get on your knees and
give it a big, mouthy kiss."

"It looks like it might bite," he said. The children
were delighted again by his response.

"Come on," Clarice insisted. "They've never seen
you make love to me."

The suggestion changed the mood immediately in at
least three of them. "Oh, please, yes," Maria begged.
"For my birthday, please?" Whatever else she had
learned in little more than a year with them, it was
certain she had been taught to indulge any sexual
appetite occurring to her. She toyed with Ramon at the
thought of just such a performance before them, reawakening in him what had been lost to laughter.

Urban blessed the champagne. It was the only alcohol he knew of which stimulated rather than eliminated
him. He gave her a perfunctory kiss and then went
behind her, inviting her to back into the steep rise of
his cock. Slowly, as they watched fascinated, he moved
himself clockwise into the deep well of her, clutching
the folds of her buttocks like handles as he burrowed
deeper into the rear approach to her.

Taking a cue from them, a simmering Maria positioned herself the same way, pulling Ramon into her,
her slender body rocking to and fro over the acute
angle of his cock, savoring each millimeter as though
her depth was being calibrated. She was a born com-
petitor, even against the token challenge of token
motherhood. When the milky coagulation of him finally
settled in and about her, the runoff streaking the
smooth track of a thigh, she turned again to watch with

undiminished interest the effort of parent one against and into parent two.

The night was long and loose, filled with imaginary rainbows constructed by champagned eyes peering into the glitter of bay life. All cares seemed to have vaporized in the explosions of tiny wine bubbles. Life, for the time, had only the purpose of rebuilding another passion and fulfilling it.

Hours had passed since Urban threw Maria against the ship's wheel in a classic calendar pose, ramming her with the last of his full potency, comeless but nevertheless satisfying to him. He lay spent and snoring on the bridge when Clarice came to Maria finally to bestow a ceremonial kiss. "Girls kiss each other, too," she said in explanation as Ramon watched.

In all her dizziness, Maria resisted at first, locking her legs against the thrust of Clarice's head when it became apparent the kiss was to be prolonged. But she weakened quickly, accepting the tongue tracings along her thighs with a mixture of resignation and expectation, scissoring her legs wide, unfurling the red and pink flag of her gender, displaying the looseness she had been taught, submitting to the directions of one of her teachers.

Her attacker was not the woman she had known, a stranger even to herself, her mind detached by the erosive force of alcohol. She paused only a moment in her lost pursuit, her tongue thick with the liquor of grapes and the liqueur of libido, to instruct another of her pupils. "Go up me," she motioned to Ramon. "Up the back."

It was a night lost to memory for her, a night closer to hallucination than reality. But it had been there and fragments of it would stick forever in the mesh of her mind as well as those of the other participants.

A sense of remoteness, of isolation, overtook Giles in the aftermath of the birthday party. He was beyond shame, distant even from remorse, but hangovers did induce a measure of paranoiac uneasiness and restlessness. Dawn's natural optimism only heightened his feeling of estrangement from reality.

The children remained locked in a desperate sleep, exhausted but unable to maintain the coma of slumber long enough to overcome their champagne sickness. An aroma of stale vomit resisted the cleansing breezes curling through the cabin, clinging to their naked bodies like some diabolic perfume.

He pressed the starter button after hauling in the anchor, setting the cruiser's engine into immediate vibration. But no one rose in spite of the noise and tremors. Clarice, like the children, lay nude and spent in an adjoining cabin, her illness contained but pressing painfully outward throughout her body. Urban, by contrast, felt no worse and no better than he felt most mornings. He was accustomed to the seminausea of overindulgence. He accepted it as normal, enduring its distress with the knowledge it would recede gradually during the day.

The boat sliced sharply into the bay's indigo crepe, making a neat surgical incision as he spun the wheel shoreward. His eyes had been casually seeking the elegant white profile of the *Andromeda* ever since their arrival. Now they roamed the horizon with a new urgency. They were entering their third day in Acapulco, their sixth since fleeing Los Angeles. It was not an indefinite vacation. It was not really a vacation at all.

He squirmed within the tight clutch of his slacks, the head of his penis raw and sensitive from the strenuous efforts of the night. His hand sought it deftly, easing it into a less irritating position next to the opposite thigh. His thoughts were far removed from sex, distant even from familial matters. He was unashamed of the brooding concern he felt for his own welfare. Selfishness, he reminded himself, was a key motivating force in success.

"Easy!" the elderly man called from the end of the pier. "Cut your engine!"

He did as he was told, feeling the slap of backwash as the blades stopped biting the soupy dock water. The boat nosed against the weathered timber buffering the pier and nuzzled a cluster of pilings before he was able to secure lines fore and aft.

"Got to be careful, *señor*," the man warned, shaking his head as he talked.

"I'm getting the hang of it," Urban replied defensively. He peered into the narrow passageway, seeing the bodies stirring but not arising. To hell with them, he thought. Let them figure out where he was going and what he was up to.

"Say, *amigo*," he said, leaping awkwardly onto the pier. "Do you know the Kimberley yacht?"

"*Sí.*"

"Where's it tied up these days?"

The old man shrugged. "If it in Acapulco, it always right there." He pointed a gnarled finger toward the center of the bay.

Urban wanted to dismiss the man's assumption because it interfered with his plans and conflicted with his wishes. But the man had no reason to be misleading him. "How long's it been gone?" He tried to sound nonchalant.

"Let's see." The hands looked arthritic as he counted, bent into permanent angles that made them look like claws. "Maybe twelve, maybe thirteen days," he said finally.

"I'm a friend of the owner," Urban lied. "Any idea when he's due back?"

The old man grinned, revealing a scattered assortment of uneven brown teeth. "He's reech. He do what he like."

Urban persisted. "He must have other friends around here. They'd know his schedule, wouldn't they?"

"He throw parties all the time. Every day. But those people, they come only wintertime. Who they, I dunno."

"Damn," Urban said, a welter of emotions summed up in a single word.

"You know something?" the old man said, lowering his voice and glancing about as though revealing a deep secret. "Ever seence papers show him playing with leetle girls, he run away."

Of course, Urban thought. The photos of Kimberley with Maria in *Tartarus* must have caused a sensation in Acapulco society. The millionaire was not a recluse, but he was also not renowned as a playboy. The new image must have embarrassed him into flight.

The act of revelation seemed to stimulate the dockman, at least verbally. He insisted on offering an appraisal of the situation. "You see that leetle girl? She so preety! I theenk he fuck her."

Urban could not help reflecting on the lascivious nature of gossip. Repetition hardened it into fact, which in turn was embellished by each individual's own conceptions and fantasies. Even though he accepted it as truth, his present source was making a gossip speculation and he therefore rejected it. "I don't think so, *amigo,*" he said. "A man with his money doesn't have to do such things." Later, as he sought a newsstand, he smiled inwardly at his own specious logic.

In the lobby of one of the larger hotels he found an exceptionally sophisticated newspaper and magazine display, including dailies from all the major North and South American cities. He scooped up the *Los Angeles Times* and the *Herald-Examiner* immediately, scanning the remainder of assorted periodicals as he waited to pay the vendor. His looping gaze was suddenly pulled taut by the cover of a Spanish magazine, *Ole!,* with a full-page closeup of Maria—embracing Kirk Kimberley and Keith Avery. He dove for the pile, at first lifting all of the dozen or so copies, then deciding such a confiscation would be too obvious. Instead, he limited himself to three, pushing them along with the papers to the woman behind the counter.

In the coffee shop, where he managed to induce a waitress to slip a liberal splash of tequila into his cup, the same girl responded to a five-dollar bill for her services as a translator. The article, accompanied by shots he had not seen before, was written in florid Spanish prose, heavy with innuendo but carefully avoiding any explicit charges. After all, Mexico was a moralistic, Catholic-dominated country officially frowning upon hanky-panky, even among consenting adults. The suggestion that a visiting tycoon might possibly be enjoying the favors of an underage girl of Mexican derivation was daring beyond belief. The waitress summed it up at the conclusion of her rendition of the piece. "He's a peeg if he do that," she said. By agreeing, he succeeded in gaining a second cup of spiked coffee, quieting the trembling of his hands sufficiently so that he could hold the newspapers in front of him rather than flat on the crowded table.

Once again his eyes were pulled back sharply by something they had passed. The caption in the *Los Angeles Times* stated simply:

ADOPTION LAWYER CHARGED

The story below it was brief, in keeping with the *Times*'s rather sedate approach to potentially sensational news. He skipped rapidly to the more flamboyant Hearst newspaper, riffling its pages until he came upon a four-column banner heralding a much longer account of the same story. In extra-bold Bodoni type, it proclaimed:

ADOPTION ATTORNEY RAN BABY MILL, D.A. CLAIMS

It mattered little to Urban Gilles that he was learning the true nature of Pacific Place for the first time. Avery had actually induced pregnant girls to forego abortions—for a fee of course—in order to assure him of a continuing supply of infants for adoption. The demand was nationwide, the article stated, with newborn babies commanding five-figure prices. It was a lucrative business for the dashing attorney, who until now had been able to skirt legalities and avoid investigations with both skill and liberal revenue-sharing among top officials. The bribe charges were being submitted to a grand jury, the story continued, along with a variety of other allegations, among which were contributing to the deliquency of minors and operating a public shelter in a lewd and wanton manner.

Urban's eyes dropped hungrily into the lower reaches of the article. It ran down an entire column before jumping into shorter paragraphs under the breadth of the caption. There was only a passing mention of the fund-raising aspect of Avery's operations and no reference at all to Urban Giles. They likely had not yet dug into it, he decided. He was too much of a pragmatist in business matters to believe his role would not eventually be discovered and exploited by the press.

"What kind of girls, what manner of female, could be persuaded to violate maternal instincts so totally as to submit to a kind of assembly-line production of children to be abandoned by them at birth?" the article pondered piously. "Investigation officials, assisted by Daniel Tarradash of the County Department of Adoptions, say a majority of the young women at Pacific Place were either prostitutes seeking a brief respite from their profession or homeless and runaway girls from all over the nation lured to the area by dreams of motion picture careers. . . ."

He tore the story out raggedly, crumpling the rest of the paper onto the chair next to him. Avery might think of Acapulco in his attempts to target Giles and alert authorities to search for him there. He had no idea of what charges might be filed against him, if any, but he knew of the potentials and they froze his blood despite the rising heat of the day. Hurriedly, he shoved several bills under his cup and strode out into the bright sunshine toward the pier.

There would be no confrontation—followed by a rewarding compromise—with Kirk Kimberley as he had so eagerly anticipated during the long descent from Los Angeles. It was more than another disappointment. He was, for the time at least, drained of ideas. And weary. Very weary. The tiredness seemed to melt his bones, causing an internal limpness foreign to the normal alertness of his mind and body. His pace slowed as the realization of his dilemma capped the terminals of his nerves. He stared absently, longingly, into the empty cavern of a hotel lounge, then quickened at the sight of a man bobbing up from behind the bar. Could it be open so early? Or was it just a mirage, populated by the wistfulness of imagination? He stepped to the threshold and called out, "Open for business?"

The man behind the rattan bar smiled pleasantly. "*Si, señor*. Welcome."

Some solidity returned to him at the unexpected invitation. Even the largest problems could be somewhat diminished by a few timely cocktails. "A very, very dry Americano-gringo martini," he said as charmingly as his mood permitted.

"I make it all gin if you like."

"No, no. That tiny bit of vermouth just seems to do something essential to it." He smiled broadly, wanting to befriend the dark bartender who was rescuing him from despair.

"Since you are my first customer of the day, I let you add your own vermouth."

"How nice of you, *amigo*," Urban said, employing once again one of the few Spanish terms in his vocabulary. He tipped the bottle slightly, quickly, into the mixing glass, hardly more than a drop easing over the rim of its neck. The bartender smiled knowingly, thrashing his spoon with professional ferocity into the mixture of ice cubes and liquor, creating a brief, silvery turbulence. Then he poured the contents through a strainer into a long-stemmed glass.

"Good luck," the bartender said. "The first of the day is my pleasure to buy you, sir."

He sat there after that and let the day invade him. The bar had a twilight illumination against the gold rush of morning. By noon it alloyed in his eyes and a sense of timelessness surrounded him. He could be anywhere. He had to keep reminding himself he was in Acapulco, unemployed.

There was a changing of shifts at three, a new, fresh Mexican replacing the man he now knew as Carlos. They had discussed everything over the course of nearly six hours. At its conclusion, he dug into his white twills and fished out ten dollars for him. "You are a fine man, Carlos," he said as he handed it to him.

"*Gracias, señor,*" Carlos said, disappearing before the last syllable had died.

The day was a fluid mass from then on. By the time he left the bar, the atmosphere had turned aluminum, everything beyond the window streaked with burnished gray. It no longer mattered that he was hunted and alone. "One more once," he said thickly to the strange new man behind the rattan barrier.

"I theenk you need some rest, *señor*," he said. "I theenk you have enough."

Urban stared blankly at him for several minutes. Then, submerging the hostility he felt, he wove out of the bar, into the aging day he had left in its youth.

"They're gone!" she greeted him, the sockets of her eyes crimson, the pupils a red mulch. All color beyond that had drained from her face, like dye in a cheap garment. Life had avalanched for her, sliding down her face, leaving deep ridges in its wake. Until now, the decline had been gradual. But now, with a terrible suddenness, the cutting edge had penetrated, plowing up planted emotions, ripping away the carefully nurtured cover growth. It was all weeds all of a sudden, all ravished earth.

"Don't worry," he said automatically. "Everything will be all right."

She thrust a scrawled note into his hands. Without reading, he could recognize the laboriously contrived penmanship of Maria. He had evolved his own signature the same way, creating it out of the writings of a cross-section of successful men. He was inordinately proud of it—its boldness, its masculinity, its individuality.

"They ran away, Urb," she said slowly, deliberately, hoping to penetrate his fog.

"I'll talk to them when they come back," he said.

She moaned in resignation. "Read it," she said.

"Dear Mommy and Daddy Giles," it began. "Ramon and I have to go away. I am going to have a baby. I want it and I want to keep it this time. We are going to get married. I love him and I want to stay with him always. Someday we will see you. I hope. Love, Maria."

Beneath her words, in the rough scrawl he had never quite learned to refine and control, Ramon added his own brief sentiments. "Thank you for being nice to us. Ramon."

He held it tightly after reading it, wrinkles forming in the paper against the force of his thumb. It was unbelievable. All of it. Everything from the moment they had been conceived, not in the womb with the magic combination of sperm and ovum, but in the fertility of his imagination, from the tinder of lust and knowledgeability, of secrecy and daring. Now they were gone.

"They're only children," he said. And then he embraced her and held her tightly and they wept together.

Chapter Eighteen

They crawled back up into the north of Mexico, taking a center route this time, through the Guadalupe Mountains, crossing the border near the Carlsbad Caverns of New Mexico. Two weeks of waiting in Acapulco, first in fashionable hotels, finally in a guest house with shared bath facilities, had produced no results, no contact from the missing children. It was impossible to notify the police without risking their own security. And so they had been forced to conduct their own feeble investigations, develop their own leads, and finally retreat before their funds gave out entirely.

The old man on the dock where they had rented the boat became their last liaison, the only person Urban entrusted with the task of keeping an eye out for the children. He could be reached at the clam house adjacent to the pier where he worked. It was a shabby denouement, perhaps the final ending, to their brief experience in parenthood and it poisoned the emotions of both of them.

"The thing is," Urban declared somewhere along the brittle route north, "we're not really bad people, Clare. We just did what anybody else would have done. I don't care what anybody says, we're just not that bad as people."

It was an odd rationalization they employed. Desire translated into deed was less than either taken separately, it contended. It was a time for being philosophical, for there was little else to occupy them except apprehension and concern. Urban simply refused to be defeated in spite of everything. His eyes, like sieves, strained out the impurities he witnessed; his mind spooned off unpleasant facts and coated them with sweet fiction. "Every man is attracted to young girls. Every woman is attracted to young boys. Nobody likes old meat. Nobody eats old vegetables." He could justify every move he had made in life and he seemed to do just that as they wove their way through the parched mountains, trying vainly to chart a future for themselves.

After days of monosyllabism, she entered his driving

trance with a quick incision. "You've got to change your name, Urb," she said. She knew of his pride in his name, in its uniqueness, in the lofty professional reputation he imagined it embodied. But she could cater to his vanity no longer. They were hunted people, lost people, possibly even demented people. That thought had occurred to her more often with the sharp slants of memory, twisted grotesquely by the overall inferno of her mind in recalling the last moments of the birthday party. But no matter. Survival had become paramount once more. They could not chance operating again under the old UGA trademark.

He did not reply immediately. In fact, he did not comment on her suggestion until the following day— after they had pulled off the road and registered at a remote hotel edging what appeared to be another desert. There was no bar there, but he had taken the precaution of buying several bottles of liquor earlier.

He was halfway through one of them when he announced clearly and evenly: "Say hello to Herb Gale."

She understood immediately. "That's good. Herb sounds like Urb. Gale is pretty close, too. If either of us slips, nobody'll be absolutely sure."

He tapped the side of his head to indicate the quality of its contents. "Urban's gone suburban at last," he jested with little enthusiasm.

Five days passed before they finally arrived in Albuquerque. The first move of Herb Gale, alias Urban Giles, was to buy every west coast newspaper he could find as well as the local papers. There was nothing in any of them concerning anything which interested him. Except, of course, the help-wanted ads in the Albuquerque editions. He brooded over these with a mounting sense of futility.

"I'm not qualified for any of these goddam jobs," he complained. "Not that I want any of them." He paced the room for a time, then put his hand on the doorknob. "I'm going out. I've got to get out for a while."

She was too exhausted to make any serious objection. "Don't get drunk, Urb. Please?"

He found a bar several doors down from the hotel. It was a considerable comedown after Acapulco. But they did serve booze there and booze is what he sought. He ordered a double gin instead of a martini, remembering the terror of his experience in Hollywood. The place and the clientele bore some faint resemblance to that infamous spot and the slight similarity momentarily unnerved him. But then, thirst overcame hesitation and he soon forgot the scars of the past.

Within an hour, he was involved in a lengthy, rambling conversation with the only other man in the place wearing a business suit and tie. "I'm in land," the stranger said after they had probed one another tentatively for ten or fifteen minutes. "You strike me as a man who could do well in my business."

Urban was open to all offers. He listened attentively as the man outlined the prospects in selling desert real estate at heavy commissions. It had overtones of swindle about it, at least slightly flexed credibility factors, but that only heightened rather than detracted the new Herb Gale's fitting like custom-made skin over the old Urban Giles. They made a date to meet again in the same place that Friday.

It provided just the modicum of excuse he needed to turn the occasion into a small party. By the time he returned to the hotel, Clarice was asleep, the radio blaring Western music loudly enough to cover his entry. He undressed and slipped into bed, falling asleep before his head had fully settled on the pillow, visions of land booms occupying much of its empty acreage.

Clarice had long ago been eviscerated by him, hollowed out, backbone reduced to pulp, her individual spirit broken in the effort to stay in the race with her husband. It was true, she had gradually accepted his sexual propositions, even eventually enjoying the physical abandon of some of the situations that had resulted. After all, she reasoned, she was human and she could be erotically aroused in spite of misgivings. So could anyone, she argued.

But now, strangely, she missed Ramon and Maria for what they represented to her maternally, as a family, as the completion of a small circle of their own. The last night together had been a terrible mistake. She could not even begin to review it consciously without becoming ill, convinced it had precipitated their disappearance, fearful it had estranged them forever.

The numbing ride over the hot chest of Mexico had been temporarily therapeutic, sedating her senses, emptying her thoughts. Now in the hotel, accepting his intent to remain in Albuquerque, the buried fears slowly uncovered and spread out about her, demanding to be faced.

She was the first to find employment—as a sort of combination secretary-receptionist-clerk in a local insurance agency. Since she could offer no references, using the excuse of long housewifery, the manager asked her to submit to an impromptu typing and dictation test. Her performance was dazzling—at least by Albuquerque standards—and she was hired immediately. "Meet Clare Gale, girl secretary," she greeted Urban that night. "Girl?" he responded cheerily. "Oh, yes, I'd almost forgotten about the shave."

His barroom proposition, unlike so many others, did materialize. It was really an offshoot of the boiler room fraternity and there in New Mexico members of that special breed were not so readily obtainable. After all, land speculation salesmen were not that easy to find anywhere—not those who understood the special hustle necessary to sell pieces of dreams in the form of arid, undeveloped plots of land virtually in the middle of nowhere. But Herb Gale was a natural. He was in his element, if not exactly his environment, and they began, bit by bit, to prosper again.

Urban called the old man on the dock almost every time he became intoxicated, which was as often as always. Which was often. There was never any word, never any change in the situation. Additionally, he had subscribed to the Los Angeles papers by mail to follow the progress of the actions against Keith Avery. These, too, seemed stalemated—entangled by all the delaying techniques of a clever attorney suffering the grim turnabout role of defendant.

They moved out of the hotel after several months, into a garden apartment. Herb Gale was already in the process of becoming a minor legend in the real estate world of New Mexico as the result of his spectacular sales totals. He had an undeniable flair for painting the painted desert whatever color most appealed to prospective investors. "Such a nice man," the elderly in particular invariably described him to his bosses.

Perhaps at last, in this most unlikely place, they were going to take root, Clarice thought. There were even moments after a while when the elusive spark of happiness ignited her for an hour, an evening, a day. They talked occasionally of the past, wondering of the fates of Lederer and Ruth Fuller and the others whose paths they had intersected; seldom, almost never, of Ramon and Maria. The wounds were still too fresh upon her, still not cauterized despite the long numbness.

It was a compromise with a dream for both of them. She accepted that, hoping he did also. Perhaps she should have known more certainly, perhaps he was unknowable. But she did know that nothing died within him; it only lay dormant until its season came again.

"I've been sizing up this town, Clare," he announced on the eve of his fifty-third birthday. "It's perfect for a telethon. Perfect. There's a spirit of civic pride here we could turn into a real dollar-factory. Not too far from Vegas and Hollywood either, so talent wouldn't be much of a problem. . . ."

She let him ramble, crushing the tiny shoots of insecurity already seeded and rising within her. He was drinking—perhaps this, too, would pass like the fluids running through his body, forgotten once they ran their course.

Only a week later he brought a strange, coppery man to the apartment. "Clare, this is Larry Raintree," he said genially. At the mention of the name she noticed the steep rise of his cheekbones and the strong black hair and realized he was an Indian.

"A pleasure to meet you, Mr. Raintree," she said.

"Thank you. It is equally my pleasure, Mrs. Gale."

"Larry's got exciting news for us," Herb Gale said in the most enthusiastic manner of one Urban Giles. "He's going to recommend us as foster parents for two Indian children from his reservation." His face was incandescent as he spoke, the parchment of it somehow smoothing and turning translucent, the light of youth seeming to rise once more within it.

"A boy and a girl," Raintree said warmly. "Just as you specified."

"What do you say to that, Clare? How about that? You and I with our very own children at last!"

Tears rimmed her eyes and spilled down her face. Only she could know where they had come from and why. And she was not at all certain herself. Not at all.

"I'm overwhelmed," she said softly.

The end was like the beginning, one swallowed by the other, endless, continuing, like a circle. It was life as he had designed it, as she had chosen to live it with him. The hair would grow back in the valley and there would be another girl and another boy and they would begin again, like Chinese rings, another circle interlocking with the one before it. After all, they were only aspiring to the American promise of life, liberty and the pursuit of happiness.